MICHELLE RENE

MANUFACTURED WITCHES

Black Rose Writing | Texas

ISBN: 978-1-68433-179-6
PUBLISHED BY BLACK ROSE WRITING
www.blackrosewriting.com

Printed in the United States of America
Suggested Retail Price (SRP) $16.95

Manufactured Witches is printed in Garamond

Dedicated, in loving memory, to Dr. Nina Simone.

MANUFACTURED WITCHES

CHAPTER ONE

Gently the train rocked back and forth as it trekked through the countryside. The cadence was a calming one, and many a traveler fell asleep in its embrace. After a while, even the sudden bumps and jolts of some bit of wood or rock on the track felt normal. A body could absorb the impact without much thought at all.

Perhaps that's why I didn't feel the tugging at first. Just another bend in the track or debris. Gentle rumbles one became accustomed to. What gave the game away eventually was the sudden relief of open air on my foot. My socks, long worn holes in each one, were suddenly exposed. Well, at least one was. For the time being, the other stayed put.

I awoke but didn't open my eyes. No need yet to let them know I had cottoned on; not until I knew what the game was exactly. One shoe was off, and they were working on the other one.

"Don't figure I can fit into these boots. They awful small," said one whispered voice.

"No matter. Better than nothin'. We can cut the toes to make room," whispered his gruff companion.

In a smooth movement, I lifted my head and my pistol to the men in front of me. The cocking of the hammer stopped them mid-thievery. I tipped my hat back to take them in full. Two grown men they were and sorry sights at that. All worn and ragged from riding the boxcars too long. Perhaps, in a few decades, that would be me. I shook off the thought and aimed my pistol straight. They held their hands high in surrender.

"You best hand that back to me."

One man stepped forward and kicked the boot back in my direction. I examined their feet. One wore mismatched shoes, if you could call them shoes. The other had no shoes at all. Just socks with more holes in them than mine.

"You best go red light yourselves. I don't mean to ride this train with one eye open," I said without the even the smallest hint of doubt in my voice.

"Come on, kid. We didn't mean nothin'," said the one in socks.

"Yeah, we need some shoes. You can see the state we're in."

"Seeing as how I more or less share that state, I'm going to decline. Off with you."

"You can't be more than sixteen or seventeen. Puny at that if you don't mind me sayin' it. Surely you got someone at home waiting fer you. Me and ole Marv here ain't got no one."

"I don't mind you sayin', but I do mind your presence. I ain't got anyone waiting for me, same as you. You tried to steal from me. This is your last warnin' before I start letting bullets fly. Go to the door and escort yourselves out."

"You can't mean that. Train ain't even slow enough to jump. It's a good chance we'll die or get real banged up at least."

I turned the gun to point at the man with the mismatched shoes. He stiffened when the barrel leveled directly at him. It was an unblinking sort of death staring his way.

Without another word, he moved the few feet to the boxcar door. He shoved the heavy thing and slid it to the side. The world rushed past us in a blur of trees and land. What might be green in the daylight was blue and dark in the night. Night colors like that spoke of evil things.

A tingle in my gut said this thing I was doing was wrong, but I ignored it. Not much else to do now. I was bone tired, and they were desperate enough to try to steal from me my only pair of boots. For the last three days, I'd been awake and travelling in fear of this very thing or worse. Sleep was a necessity now, and this was my only way to ensure it.

His buddy joined him at the door. They both looked out into the whirring landscape.

"This is on your head, son. If something happens to us. It's on you," said the man with the mismatched shoes.

Both men turned and leapt out of the car and into the blur of the world passing by me.

"No, it ain't," I said to a now-empty boxcar.

Perhaps later I would feel bad for this. It was probable. Never did I pride myself on cruelty. If anything, I normally strove for kindness. For now, I couldn't afford a conscience. Besides, what curse could come from a ragged heap like that?

I was so tired. Too tired even to get up and slide the door shut. A dumb move if there ever was one. It just invited trouble, but the lure of sleep convinced me otherwise. Now that the imminent danger had passed, I slumped back against the dense hay that had become my temporary bed. The car had been mostly empty when I boarded, a good reason to choose it. No one would be checking an empty car. At least not at first.

It was normally used for livestock. That fact was undeniable. The odor of breath and feces still lingered even though no animals stood around me. In the board below, stamped hoof prints told stories of cattle.

The hay acting as my bed was sparse and sour smelling at that. It had to have been a good while since this train carried something living. At least since before the last rainfall seeing as the bottom portions of hay were mildewing. I couldn't recall the last rain I'd witnessed myself, but then again, the train had probably seen a good bit more than me.

I didn't mind the smell, not with the promise of sleep tugging me down. I pulled on my errant boot and fell back into the hay. Somewhere beneath me, I thought I heard the skitter of insects. Tiny snaps in the fibers of my bed. A whispering.

Let them crawl over me, I thought. I don't care. Nothing that small matters anymore. Just please let me sleep if for only a little while.

When the train stopped in Amarillo, I nearly was caught. The station men moved from car to car, readying the cargo for unloading. Normally, I would have heard them or felt the train stop. My person would sneak away and blend with the nearest town. But my bones were tired. The deep sleep I had fallen into held me captive. It wasn't until I heard the men shouting a few box cars down from mine that I awoke with the urgency the moment required.

"Get out of there, you lazy bums! I mean it. I'll call the sheriff. You have to the count of five to move it. After five, I let loose the dogs on you."

I sat bolt upright. Somewhere nearby dogs barked that choked sort of sound, strained by the pull of their leashes.

"One...Two..."

Shoving my pistol into the gunny sack I carried, I scrambled to my feet and made my way to the door. When I looked down the line, the men with the dogs were four cars down from mine.

"Three...Four..."

I leapt to the ground and ran the opposite direction. A few of the dogs turned and barked at me, straining to follow. No use turning to look. There was no way to go but forward. The last thing I heard as I ran into the waking morning was the man with the dogs laughing.

"Your comrade over there has the right idea. Run for your life."

Amarillo stretched out before me as I made it out of the train yard and into the city proper. Bustling it was and big. Too big for my comfort. It was a cow town; no doubt there. The scent of manure and burned rawhide drifted on the wind. Grit and what I hoped was dirt stung my eyes and stuck in my teeth. There was something more here though. A pull I couldn't label.

Lots of people who rode the rails stayed in big towns like this. They panhandled and worked odd jobs as long as they could. Then, off they went on another train going nowhere special. I had ridden long enough to know it wasn't for me. Really, the life wasn't good for anyone. Constantly living in fear, running for your life at every stop. I didn't want it, not long term. I was young. I could work. The thing of it was work was hard to find. The dust had come in a few years ago and buried the world as we knew it. Farms choked, and so did the people.

When Mamaw passed, there was nothing left for me to do but ride the rails. Banks took the house and the land. No family left to take me in. Even if there were, who'd want me? It wasn't a lie I told the men the night before. I truly had no one left.

Amarillo had potential for sure. It was big enough to have restaurants and hotels. I could get a job washing dishes like I had in previous towns. Maybe one of the ranch hands could put in a word for me with the boss man. Animals never scared me much.

As I walked along the streets, that idea faded away. There were throngs of people slumped against buildings and hiding in alleyways. Most were begging. I walked by business after business, and most had signs in their windows.

No Jobs. Don't Ask.
You Pay, or You Leave.
Panhandlers Prosecuted.

The work here was dried up. That was clear enough. There would be nothing here for me, but hope was not lost yet. I made my way to a general store that seemed to be doing a brisk bit of business. Several farmers in wagons and trucks congregated in the back lot hoping to sell and barter with what they had.

I smelled sweet tobacco as I got closer along with the tang of manure. Keeping to the shadows of the building, I spied on the men as they talked and laughed with one another. One man traded the store's owner a sack of potatoes for some sugar and coffee. Another bought his supply with eggs and two hens.

The man with the hens walked back to his truck with the provisions he had bought. I followed him but hid in and among the other vehicles. One look at me and anyone would peg me as a boxcar kid. With that label came disdain. The picture of a delinquent youth who would probably rob you blind if you gave them an inch.

There was no point in offering my services there with the way I looked. Amarillo was thick with people like me, but perhaps where this fellow was from that wasn't the case. After all, he had a stack of crates four or five feet high in the back of his truck. Half the crates were occupied with chickens. Pretty fat hens too. Wherever he called home might be faring better. No train stops would mean fewer boxcar kids. I might have a chance at a job there.

He sucked on a cigarette and gabbed with another man. The one with the potatoes.

"I tell you, it is a beating coming up here all the way from Tanglewood," said the chicken man.

"Why make the trek? Your man there not buying eggs?" asked the potato man.

"Norman's flush with eggs. He's bartering less and less these days. Fewer customers and all that. Says it's hard for him to buy supplies we can't provide. Wants money."

"Don't we all? Is it so bad you're selling your laying hens?"

"Not yet. I keep the best at home. These are the old gals. Good for the bellies more than the eggs. Past their prime."

The men conversed more or less this way for another fifteen minutes. I took that time to sneak around the truck, hiding my purple shadow among the shadows of the wheels. The sun was still young, making the shadows long. It made it easy to blend in with the darkness of things.

When I managed to get around to the back of the truck, the tailgate was already up. Such a break for me. I tossed my gunny sack into the back of the truck and followed after it just as fast. I had to be quiet. The presence of my sudden weight lowered the truck slightly, but not enough to notice. I squeezed myself down in the small break in between the two rows of chicken crates.

It was a tight fit. I was barely able to squeeze my whole body there. The gunny sack was on top of me as an added barrier between me and anyone who might look inside. I didn't mind the closeness. There was a kind of security in it. However, the chickens didn't agree. They squawked and flapped their wings in protest. Feathers flew this way and that. I had to blow them away from my face. I hissed at them as quiet as I could manage. They were not impressed. One particularly agitated hen pecked at my leg from her crate. I bit my lip to not cry out and give away the game.

"Pipe down in there!" shouted the chicken man from outside the truck. He banged his fist against the fender of the truck. "You keep that up, and I'll ring your necks myself when we get back to Tanglewood."

As if understanding him, the hens calmed slowly. Even the one pecking my leg stopped her painful campaign. I heard the men say their goodbyes as the chicken man walked around to the front of the truck. The vehicle slumped forward with his sudden weight, and he fired up the engine. Before I knew it, we were on the road. The only thing I could see above me was blue sky and errant feathers.

I hadn't ever heard of Tanglewood, but I hoped it was beautiful.

CHAPTER TWO

I woke to someone kicking my feet. Jolting upright, the first thought that came to me was the sense of still sleeping in the train. The boxcar men were back somehow and trying to steal my boots again. When my eyes adjusted, it was daylight in an open sky. There was no jostling of the track beneath me, and a very angry farmer stared daggers at me from the other side of the tailgate.

"What do you think you're doing? I ain't handing out free rides."

"I'm sorry, sir. I ain't looking for a free ride. I will gladly work it off. Please, I need a job," I said to the chicken man.

"A job you say? That's a new one. I thought all you kids did was steal and beg."

"I aim to work, sir. My apologies for not askin' permission. I didn't think you'd let me on."

The chicken man looked me up and down, pondering my presence and the words that accompanied it. Apparently, I had made some sort of impression. Otherwise, I would be running for my life at the present moment. He held a shotgun lazily pointing down to the ground.

"Well, that's alright, I suppose. Ain't no harm as long as you didn't steal any eggs or nothin'."

"No, sir. I didn't touch the hens. They touched me though. The one over here pecked me up a good bit in the beginning. Almost bloody."

He smiled. Even chuckled a little.

"Yeah, she's one to do that. Listen here boy, I ain't got no work for you. Got seven children of my own that work the farm. Hard enough feedin' those. I won't charge you fer the ride. You seem nice enough. You got any family to speak of?"

"No, sir."

"I see. Hop down from there."

I did as instructed. The chickens flapped a bit as I got up and jumped off the tailgate. When I stood on the ground, I was a head shorter than the man. He looked down at me, appraising the sight. Grown men always seemed unimpressed with my size.

"Here," he said holding out a nickel from his pocket.

"Sir?"

"You're skinny, kid. The good Lord wouldn't look kindly on me if I let a nice kid go hungry. Take it," he said and pointed down a dusty street toward a smattering of buildings clumped together. "There's town. Tanglewood. Your best bet for a job."

"Thank you, sir."

The chicken man nodded, and I hurried away from him, a whole nickel richer. I silently patted my own back for the decision to try things out in the country. Perhaps Tanglewood could be a home for me.

As I got closer to the main square, I saw it was a small place to be sure. Not nearly as large and bustling as Amarillo had been. While the bigger town had been teaming with people, this one's occupants were few. Farmers mostly. They made their way along the streets, some even nodded politely to me as I passed. The tugging I'd felt in Amarillo was stronger here. There was no deciphering what it was, but I was getting closer.

I made my way to the heart of every town, the general store. Everything always revolved around the general store. I hadn't eaten much of anything in a couple of days. The first thing on the list was to get some food. Tanglewood's general store sat at a large corner lot on the west side of the square. As I made my way there, the promise of food tugged at my insides.

My hand was reaching for the door handle when I saw her. Down the road a piece and just outside the main thoroughfare was the strangest sight I had ever seen. There was an old hitching post, broken in places but the main part still stood true. It wasn't the post that was odd. It was the girl chained to it. She was a slip of a thing with a metal chain around her waist that fastened around the sturdy part of the post. Above her was a sign.

Thou Shalt Not Suffer a Witch

I gave up the idea of the general store for a moment and made my way to her. Such an odd sight. A whole town walking about and doing their business, yet they ignored this girl. Pretended she wasn't there. As I got closer, I saw she was about my age if not a tad younger. Hard to tell things like that when a creature cowered in chains. Her lips were chapped, and her skin was dry from sitting out in the sun. A burlap sack of some sort loosely fitted around her like a dress. I couldn't help but wonder how long she had been out here.

"Miss? Miss, are you alright?"

The girl didn't acknowledge me, not at first.

"Miss? Is there something I can do for you?"

When she finally tilted her head up at me, she did so sluggishly. Great hazel eyes looked up into mine. Her dirty hair had probably been golden once. Now, it was dry and oily at the same time, sticking in clumps and gathering in knots around her face. She shook her head from side to side slowly as though it caused her great pain.

"Are you sure? I can help you. Hold tight. I'll be right back."

She didn't answer. I turned on my heel and hurried back over to the general store. There was a nickel burning a hole in my pocket.

A bell dinged when I pushed the doors open. I nodded to the man behind the counter and promptly made my way through the store. Fresh food was not practical. Who knew how long I would need it to keep. I found the aisle where the jerky was kept and grabbed three rations of it. I brought the bounty to the clerk up front. He eyed me and my selection.

"You got money for this?"

I put my nickel on the counter. He nodded and went to make change. Just behind the clerk, I spotted a number of specialty items. Tobacco, coffee beans, and candy. My eyes grew wide when I spotted the peppermints. I wasn't always a fan of that flavor of candy, but it did help with the thirst when no water could be had.

"Do I have enough left over for some of that peppermint?"

He looked at me and then up at the candy on the shelf. They sat prettily, thin sticks in a glass jar. My mouth watered thinking about them.

"You have enough for four sticks."

"I'll take those too please."

"Whatever you want, son," he said as he got the jar down from the shelf.

My purchases were gathered and packed in a paper sack. He handed them to me with a strained grin. I wondered if he knew what I was from appearance. All thoughts I had about asking him for a job left my mind as he looked at me. Perhaps I smelled bad. He probably wanted me out of his store as soon as possible as to not offend his other patrons.

"Just one more thing before I'm out of your hair, sir. You got a well around here I can use to fill my canteen? I'd be much obliged."

His features softened, and what I once took as strain now read more like concern.

"You best leave that girl alone," he said gently.

"Excuse me, sir?"

"You're new here. I can tell. I saw you out there talking to her. The one with the witch sign. She's a Jones Girl. Best you leave her be. You seem nice enough. Wouldn't want trouble fer you. Stay clear of the Jones's."

"I don't understand."

The door jingled a bell as it swung open. Suddenly, the clerk straightened and smiled widely at the new costumer. He was a tall gentleman in a black suit, very modest and finely pressed. Such a fancy dark suit, it didn't seem practical for Texas. I pegged him in his fifties but well preserved at that. I had no idea a face could hold such a sour expression for so long. He looked at me sharply, and I flinched the way the clerk had.

"Why yes, young man. There's a barrel 'round back where you might fill your canteen," said the clerk with a flick of his head. "It's plenty fresh. Off with you now."

I didn't ask questions. The air in the store shivered with agitation the second the man in black walked in. Something inside me said to leave and do it fast. Nothing good could possibly follow a man like that.

I went out the back and found the water barrel. I dunked my canteen, filling it to the brim. The smart thing to do was to drink about half of it down and refill it again. I did so as quickly as possible as to not let anyone see and accuse me of taking more than my fair share. Folks would find any reason at all to push someone like me out of town.

When I made it back out to the street, there was no one around. It was as if the town took note of the man in the black suit and decided to hide in the shadows until his departure. I couldn't help but wonder what that meant. The shop clerk looked nervous when he entered. Why was that? And what did he mean by saying she was a Jones Girl?

I stood at the opposite corner as the store and chewed on a bit of jerky. It was good, salty and peppered just right. My mouth watered properly to moisten the bite as I chewed. The girl was still chained in the distance. I wanted to go back to her with the food, but something inside me said to wait. Not yet. Give it a few more minutes.

When the scary man stepped out of the store, he held a flour sack with his purchases over his shoulder. He crossed the street, pausing once to gaze down the way at the girl chained in the distance. A look of disgust covered his face. He shook his head slightly as if trying to rid himself of a foul smell. When he continued to my side of the street, I had to look away so as to not snarl at the man.

The imposing fellow left the square. Where he went, I couldn't say. All I really cared about was that he wasn't in sight anymore. As soon as he did, I made my way back to the supposed witch. Somehow she looked worse for the wear since I'd seen her only twenty minutes before. I sat beside her and leaned against the post.

"Hi. I'm back. Thought you might want a bit of food. Some water?"

She gazed up at me, her eyes still listless. When she looked at my offerings, she shook her head.

"It ain't no trouble. I don't mind sharing."

The girl made to shake her head no again, but when she saw my canteen, her eyes lit up. Her lips were so dry the bottom of them was split right opened, cracked with dried blood on it. At that point, I don't think she could resist the water if even she wanted to. I handed the canteen to her, and she greedily drank about a third of it, unable to control herself. When she handed it back, her face looked a bit chagrinned. I couldn't help but smile.

"No trouble. I can get more. Here, want some jerky?"

She considered the jerky, but it was the peppermint her eyes lit upon. There was no doubting the sparkle in them. I reached in and pulled out a stick and handed it to the supposed witch. The girl hesitated for a moment before she took it from my hands. When she bit off a piece, the joy in her face was worth all the effort in the world.

"I'm glad you like it. Like I said, I don't mind sharing."

She looked at me suddenly with an urgency. She sat up straighter, the chain around her waist rattling a bit from the movement. To my surprise, she reached her hand inside the collar of her sack of a dress. She was fiddling with something just beneath her bosom. A red blossom flushed in my cheeks. I threw my hands up in protest.

"No, no. I didn't mean that. I'm not trying to get anything like that from you. I'm just trying to help."

She stopped long enough to give me an exacerbated glare. Apparently, that was not what she intended either. When she brought her hand back out, she was holding a small sack. The paper of it was worn and crinkly only at the top. She opened it to me, and I saw it was filled with roasted pumpkin seeds. The girl held the bag out, offering me some.

"I see. You want to share too. Well, I can't say no to that."

There we sat, the most unusual of friends. A boxcar boy and a chained witch. The very epitome of outcasts nobody wanted sharing what little we had. To anyone passing, this might be absurd. Two filthy urchins more dirt than flesh to the naked eye. Yet, we sat there in the dusty morning, eating a sparse meal with one another. Possibly the strangest picnic in the history of Tanglewood, I reckoned.

CHAPTER THREE

I had no recollection of falling asleep. Perhaps that was the point of sleep. One wasn't meant to remember actually doing it until one was woken. My thoughts kept on going until they were dreams. Somewhere in between, I forgot about being awake.

It was late afternoon when I heard the boy yelling at me. I startled awake at the sound of his voice. He barked at us like a dog might.

"Hey! Hey you," he yelled at me.

I sat up straight and looked over at the girl. She was waking as well, pulling herself up from the tight ball she had been sleeping in. No fear crossed her face when she saw the boy. If anything, it was a look of love. She even smiled a little as though he were familiar.

He was taller than me, older too. Not scrawny the way I was. I would wager him to be nineteen or twenty at best. He wore a grey suit, finely pressed like the man in black earlier. Tailored to fit him, which was an odd thing in the country. The boy glared at me and shot a look of concern over at the girl next in chains.

"You okay, Poll? Did he hurt you at all?"

"Poll? Is that her name?" I asked.

He scowled at me.

"That's none of your business. Polly, did he do somethin' bad to you?"

Polly smiled and shook her head at him. With a gentle hand, she patted mine. A tender gesture and one of friendship. I smiled back at her as though we were old friends.

The boy softened, and his back relaxed. A bit of starch still hung around his collar, but the worst of the ardor was gone. I don't know why I hadn't seen it before, but he held a small sack in his hand. It looked just like the one Polly had retrieved earlier except cleaner. I wondered if this one too was filled with pumpkin seeds.

"She's fine. I don't want nothin' from her. Who are you?" I asked now that he wasn't about to pummel me in public.

"I'm Luke Jones," he said as though I should know who he was.

"Alright, Luke. What's she to you?"

"She's my sister," he snapped at me.

"Then why do you leave her here? Why is she chained to the post? Not much of a brother if you ask me."

"No one's asking you!"

He looked around suddenly as though worried someone might hear him. Polly patted my hand to cool my head. I shut my mouth with difficulty.

"I don't have much time," he said hurriedly, the ire leaving his voice.

"What's happening here? Why is she chained?"

"It was the only way."

"The only way? What the hell does that mean?"

Luke crept closer and handed the bag of seeds to Polly. When he spoke, it was quick and in a hushed tone. I couldn't fathom why. No one was near enough to hear.

"You ain't from around here. You wouldn't understand," he snapped at me.

"You're right. I don't understand. You folks here believe in witches?" I asked with a mouth full of incredulity.

"You will too if you stay long enough," he replied as serious as could be.

I looked over at Polly. She shrugged. Nothing about her appeared even remotely witchlike to me. Witches were meant to be ugly with big noses and such. Warts and flying on broomsticks. That's what the stories said anyway. What I saw was a frightened girl chained to a post.

"I don't buy it. Polly's not a witch," I said.

"*She's* not, no. It was the only way. The only way I could save her."

"Locking her to a post was the only way to save her?" I asked skeptically.

"No no. I didn't lock her here. But she has to stay here. It ain't safe…"

"Luke!" said a man's voice in the distance.

We all turned to see the man in the black suit on top of a wagon with two horses tethered to the front of it. A gaggle of women and children filled up the back along with supplies. All were dressed in grey like Luke. The women wore crisp, white bonnets despite the heat.

Luke dropped the bag in front of Polly and turned to face the wagon. In the shadow of his father, Luke trembled like a leaf.

"You know you aren't supposed to fraternize with witches. Come now or you'll get such a beating," said the man in the black suit.

"Yes father, I'm coming."

He looked back at Polly quickly with an apologetic face. She nodded to him with some quiet understanding. Luke broke away from us and ran to his family's wagon before he could be admonished any further. We watched him board the wagon and ride off in the direction of the setting sun. When they were no longer in sight, she let out a loud sigh.

"So, your name is Polly?" I asked.

Polly nodded her head.

"You don't talk?"

She shrugged.

"So, maybe you talk. You just don't want to right now?"

She nodded her tiny head.

"That's alright, Poll. I talk enough for the both of us. Everyone in this town keeps telling me I should leave you alone. The way I see it, you might need some protection. A girl in need of protection shouldn't be left alone."

I opened my gunny sack wide enough to show her the pistol resting inside. Polly peaked inside and looked at me in a way I couldn't translate.

"I don't want to stay here if you want me gone, but I would be right appreciative if you let me stay and keep watch over you. Leavin' you here just doesn't feel right. Do you mind if I stay?"

Polly shook her head.

"Alright then. That's fine by me. Now, I just hafta ask. Are you a witch, really?"

Without hesitation, she shrugged in a way that said "maybe." I snickered, and she smiled too. Truth was it didn't bother me one way or the other.

"You are just full of surprises," I said. "Just don't turn me into a frog or a newt or whatever. I like being a boy."

Polly reached the few inches to collect her brother's latest offering, and she stuffed it down the front of her dress like the last one. The chain clanked as she scooted toward me and rested her head against my chest. Instinctively, I put my arm around her. It was the closest I had been to any human being in a long time, at least one I wanted to be near.

We rested there against the post watching the sunset. Two outcasts in a world hell-bent on ignoring our existence. As the world turned purple and then blue all over, I breathed in the earthy perfume of our bodies. Dirt and dried grass wafted into my nose as I felt Polly's breaths even out and deepen into the cadence of sleep. Something told me to stay awake and vigilant. To protect her in a night full of dangers, but the long days of my past made everything heavy. It wasn't long until the comfort of a sleeping companion pulled me down into sleep with her.

CHAPTER FOUR

Time was lost to me yet again. It seemed my life of late was a series of fevered dreams book ended with rude awakenings. This proved to be the case yet again. It was definitely a trend that needed to be dealt with. When yet another voice to close for comfort startled me awake, I knew all this had to stop.

"Why isn't this nice, Johnny? A picture really. Sometimes it takes a strange fool to see a domestic folly."

When my eyes opened, there was a woman. Larger than life, she seemed. She stood over me like a giant might in a flowing dress of red and blue. Such patterns and along her skirt; I had never seen the like. Circles and angles and patterns unlike any I'd seen on a woman. Her hair too was wrapped in similar cloth like something from a fairytale. Turbans from Arabian Nights or something like that. She held the reigns to a mule twice the size of any I had seen up close. The picture didn't seem real at first as I squinted at her against the morning sky, like when you blink up at a building with the sun behind it.

It was when I looked over at Polly that I realized she was not a dream. The wiry girl stiffened all over. She stared up at the woman, tension coloring her gaze. Her limbs went rigid, and so did mine.

That was enough warning for me. I stood in an attempt to look menacing and pulled my pistol out of the gunny sack. When I stood, the woman before me no longer appeared giant. In reality, from a standing position, she wasn't much taller than I was. Still, an air revolved around her that made her grand. I pointed the pistol at her all the same even if my aim was shaky.

"We ain't doin' anything wrong, Ma'am. Let us be," I said with all the dreaded sincerity I could muster.

She merely smiled.

"Cool your heels, child. We both know that pea shooter of yours ain't loaded."

This cut me to the quick faster than anything else she could have said. I hadn't had bullets in my gun for months. A good deal of my bullets went to shooting at wild dogs or a few ill-fated attempts to kill a raccoon for dinner. Most people were so frightened by the sight of the gun, they didn't notice it wasn't loaded. Without thinking, I lowered the barrel and gawked at her.

"Oh, come now. You think a lady like me gets around in the world without knowing when a gun pointed to her head is loaded? Please, child. No need getting your back up all over again. I ain't here to hassle the two of you."

Her voice was smooth as honey, but it didn't fool me. The slickest talkers sometimes were the most dangerous.

"Then what are you here to do?" I asked as I tucked the gun into the back of my pants.

"I aim to take this little gal with me," she said with a smile.

I balled up my fists and stepped in between her and Polly.

"Relax, Galahad. You can come along too."

"Where do you want to take her?"

"To my home, silly boy."

"She ain't going nowhere she don't want to," I demanded.

The woman put her hands on her hips and squared off with me. There was something solid and sure about her. She smelled of some sort of oil made of flowers, but there was nothing delicate about her. It would take more than a breeze to knock her down. With how little I'd eaten, I wasn't sure I could hold out to more than that. Still, she relented her staring at me and trained it down to Polly on the ground.

"That's fair enough, ain't it wee one? You know who I am?"

Polly shrunk a bit and scooted closer to my legs. One small arm wrapped around my ankle. She nodded up at the strange woman.

"I see. Your pappy been tellin' you stories about Miss Camille, I suppose?"

Polly nodded her head again.

"Would it help if I said he's a rotten liar?"

Polly suppressed a grin and shrugged her shoulders.

"I reckon he's the one who put you here in these chains?"

There was no response to that one. Polly merely turned away and tried to hide behind my legs. She reached for one of my hands, and I held it.

"Do you even know what's happening here, son?" asked Camille when she looked back at me.

"No, Ma'am. Polly don't seem to talk much."

"Why're you here helping her then?"

"Because…it's the right thing to do. She needed help."

The tension was broken when Camille clapped her hands together and hooted. A huge smile broke across her face. Polly and I jumped at the sudden noise of her clapping. It was like thunder that pops out of nowhere. Her mule merely twitched an ear at the irritation.

"Hot damn! Johnny, we got us a real Galahad here. In the flesh and bones right here in Tanglewood. This is a sight to behold. Will wonders never cease?"

"I'm sorry. Who's Johnny?"

"Oh, I'm so sorry! Where are my manners?" Camille gestured to the mule at her side as though he were a person and not a beast. "Johnny Sanders, this is Polly Jones and Galahad. Polly and Galahad, this is Johnny Sanders."

I didn't really know what to say. How did one react to being introduced to a mule with a first and last name? A great inner debate raged for about thirty seconds in my mind. This woman was obviously nuts, but I didn't want to offend her in a way that meant violence. Not in my weak state. In the end, I nodded to the mule as though he were a man and tipped my hat.

We heard the general store's door jingle and heavy footfalls along the deck. When I looked over, I saw the clerk standing out on the edge of the walkway, gawking in our direction. His feet pivoted on the edge of the wood as though the earth below were on fire. He didn't dare move closer but craned his neck as far as it would go.

"Miss Camille, you do know them children is white?" he hollered in our direction.

Camille turned to look at him, shading her eyes to the sun.

"I did notice that, Norman Jackson. Thank you for the observation."

The worried look on his face deepened into an almost comical expression. He twitched as he looked up and down the streets of the square. No one was around. His fear contrasted starkly with Camille's jovial smile.

"You…you know you ain't, right Camille?" he asked.

I almost laughed. The words would be ludicrous even in a normal situation, let alone the one we found ourselves in. While Polly and I were tanned from the Texas sun, Camille was a gentle shade of brown all over. Negroes were what most called them in polite society. My grandmother had another name entirely. One I'd never use for the sour taste it left after saying it.

Camille did laugh at Norman's absurd comment, and the tension dissolved.

"Yes, Mr. Jackson. I recall. Every time I look in the mirror in fact."

"Just a friendly warnin' after last time, Camille. Just a warnin'."

"I appreciate it, sir. Consider me dutifully warned."

She waved at him, and he made his way back into the store. After the bell jingled, and he was gone, she turned her attention back to us.

"Alrighty now. Who wants to come with Miss Camille? Polly?"

She stared down at Polly who was still holding my hand. Polly trembled a little behind me. The tiny thing looked back up at the woman with an unconvinced grimace.

"Oh come now, child. As far as I can tell, you got two choices here. One, you can stay here tied to a post like a dog and sporting this lovely sack ensemble for the rest of your short days. Or two, you can come with me, and we can feed and clothe you properly as best befitting a lady of your stature. What colors do you prefer in dresses, by the way?"

I looked down at Polly, but she was just as flabbergasted by the woman as I was. Colors? Clothes for a lady of her stature? Everyone seemed to know this woman but me, but no one could predict what she would say next. Briefly, I wondered if she were a complete loony or just half of one.

"Look, child, I haven't got all day. Johnny and I need to be getting back with our supplies, and I'd rather not hang around long enough for your nasty father to spot us. I can't imagine you want to stay here, and I doubt you want him to see you talking to the likes of me."

At that, Polly jumped up from the ground to her feet. Her eyes were wide with fear as she shook her head no. Whatever she knew about this Camille woman wasn't half as bad as her father seeing her conversing with her.

"Alright then. Good decision. You will come with me then?"

Polly nodded her head and made a show about linking arm around mine. She'd go with me and me alone.

"And of course, your Galahad may come as well. We have plenty of room. What say you, Galahad?"

Truth be told, I had no idea what to say. Yesterday, all I wanted was a job and a roof over my head. Now, I didn't really know what I had gotten myself into.

One thing was for sure, I wouldn't leave Polly alone, not with anyone.

"I would work," I blurted out. "I don't mean to be a burden. I aim to work to pay for my keep. No handouts."

Camille's wide grin showed up again as she appraised me.

"Of course, child. You may work. We have no lack of work to be done, but no worries about it either. Everything is for the wind, and the wind works for us all."

"What does that mean?"

"Shhhhhh...I gotta get Johnny positioned just right. Help Polly move as far as you can get her that way."

I wrapped my arms around Polly and moved her far away from the post. We were at the end of the tether the chain provided. Camille walked the mule around so his hindquarters faced the post that held Polly to her prison. She cooed and coaxed the animal so that he was lined up a very specific distance from the post. He only snorted a bit.

"Johnny! Coyote!" she screamed and slapped the mule on the haunch.

He brayed and kicked with his back legs so hard it shattered the wooden post Polly was tied to. Splinters flew everywhere. The heavy chain fell loose to the ground.

"Well then. That worked well. You are free, my dear."

Polly moved away from me and gathered the metal links in her hands. She was free, but the chain was still wrapped around her waist.

"Never mind that, dear. You are free. We'll figure that when we get home. I would so like it if you'd call it home. The wagon's around back."

Despite all the fear we should have had, Polly and I started following the strange woman. The whole ordeal seemed straight from a storybook. The idea of ducklings blindly following their mother came to mind. The unease hit when I couldn't remember how that particular fairy tale ended.

Polly and I looked at one another, sharing silently shocked expressions. We didn't know where we were going or what would be in store for us there. In the end, anything had to be better than the post. We limped along after her, our limbs like jelly from sitting for so long. I helped Polly carry her chains to Camille's wagon. It too was painted as garishly as the woman dressed. Everything was too much all of a sudden. Too much to consume quietly.

"I'm sorry, but why are you helping us? Don't you care at all that most people in this town are convinced Polly's a witch?"

"Oh my dear boy, that doesn't bother me a bit. In fact, it's a bonafide letter of recommendation in my book. You see, I'm in the witchin' business."

"The what? What is witchin' business? Wait, who are you?"

"My name is Miss Camille Renoir Lavendou, and I guarantee that everything you've heard about me is only fifty percent exaggerated."

CHAPTER FIVE

Polly curled up in the back of the wagon among the goods and sundries. Despite the heat of the day, she couldn't seem to cease her shivering. I myself had only been sitting there at the post with her for the better part of a day. Who knew how long she'd been there. I helped Camille cut the chain with a heavy axe from her wagon. Her skinny limbs trembled when she rested them on the sacks of flour and feed. Camille threw an old quilt on top of her for comfort more than anything else.

I sat at the lead of the wagon with Miss Camille. Seemed the proper thing to do. Whomever this strange woman was, she had rescued Polly and me from a bad predicament. It was only fitting I keep her company.

The bench creaked and bowed a bit when I sat next to her as though it had been unoccupied for a while. Camille snapped the reins, and Johnny Sanders began our journey to a place I could only guess at. He grunted a bit as mules did, but set off as though he already knew the way.

"Why name your mule Johnny Sanders?" I asked her after the town was a good ways behind us. "I ain't never heard of an animal with a first and last name."

"Then you *have* heard of it?" she asked wryly.

"What? No, I said I hadn't."

"I know what you said, but saying ain't and never together cancels them out. Two negative words makes a positive. What you actually said was you had heard of it."

I pondered this. It was a thing that might have made sense if I had all my faculties about me. Truth was the world was a little fuzzy after days on the road with little food. She must have seen my confusion because she smiled and went on with her words.

"Never mind that school talk. We got time to dig there. I named him Johnny Sanders for a very strategic purpose. You see, there used to be an old drunk who stumbled about town by the name of Johnny Sanders. No one cared for him at all. He was more of a nuisance than a buffoon if you catch my meaning."

"He cause a bit of trouble?" I asked.

"Nothing terrible. He'd pilfer food and raid gardens. Stumble about hollerin' when he was drunk. That sort of thing. In the end, old Johnny just sort of disappeared. No one really knew what happened to him. Could've run off or maybe something worse. He just up and left the Earth one day."

"Then why name your mule after him? Were you close?"

"Heavens no. I hated him as much as the next person. It just so happened I bought my mule here about the same time Johnny went missing. I saw me an opportunity there. I named him Johnny Sanders, so the folks 'round here would think it was the man turned beast."

I stared at her incredulously.

"Why the hell would they think that?"

"You saw the way Polly reacted to me. Folks around here genuinely believe I'm a witch. Magic, potions, broomsticks, all of it. Best way to keep them thinking that way is to plant stories of my supposed power. They see me walking a mule named Johnny Sanders, they think he wronged me somehow, and now he's my genuine beast of burden."

"But, you didn't?"

"No. I have many peculiarities, but that ain't one of them. Best to keep the folks thinking what they will so long as they leave me alone. Superstition goes a long way to self-preservation. They know my name, but nothing solid about me. Speaking of names, I have to say I didn't catch your name, son."

"Nat," I said shortly.

"Nat, huh? I assume that's short for Nathaniel? Got a last name?"

"Not one of consequence."

"Fair enough, young Nat."

We rode in an amiable quiet for a piece. The things Camille had said swirled in my mind, and I needed a minute to try to snatch them from the air. I had so many questions, but it was best to ration my thoughts and focus rather than prattle about. A bit of food was also needed for the foggy head of mine before deep thinking was needed. The big question rattling in my mind finally came down to light on my tongue, so I decided to ask that one first.

"Polly's family. They left her there tied to the post like that. Called her a witch.

How could anyone do that to a girl?"

Camille sighed. Her dark eyes stared forward with the look of someone exhausted by the world around her. The corners of her mouth tipped downward in what I assumed was her version of a scowl.

"She's a Jones Girl. That is to say she is from the Jones colony just outside of town. The longer you're here, the more you'll hear about them."

"What sort of colony is it?"

"The unhealthy sort to be sure. Polygamists, but that ain't the real problem with them."

"I heard about that sort of thing. Mormons?"

"I reckon at one time in their history they were. I ain't got beef with real Mormons, at least, none to speak of. What I do not abide are zealots. The men in charge have made the colony somethin' cursed. They auction off young girls to older men. Their women and children live in fear. If an older boy is the least bit obstinate, they are forced to leave without supplies or money. I don't know why poor Polly back there got the treatment she did, but I guarantee it wasn't witchcraft."

"Why doesn't anyone stand up to them? Why wouldn't anyone in town help her?"

"The Jones colony owns most of everything around here. People follow their lead in all matters of business. It would be too costly to anger the elder men. You wouldn't want the Jones folks to boycott your cattle or feed or whatever."

"But you don't mind?"

Camille laughed out loud. Hers was a whole-hearted laugh. Nothing held back in it. It was the way children laughed. Johnny Sander's ears twitched.

"I don't need them for anything. I am not beholden to anyone. The Jones men don't scare me a bit. Bullies, the lot of them. Trust me, a bully's weakness is his own fear, and they are all terrified of the witch Camille."

We passed the time gently along the dusty road on the way to somewhere unknown to me. The path we took was less a road than a trail marked by the parallel lines where wagons or trucks might cut into the ground. The land around us was prairie; a rolling ocean of dried grass speckled with a scraggly tree here and there. There was the gentle scent of sweet grass on the breeze, even though the hot Texas sun baked everything amber.

It wasn't until we reached the sign that I noticed the difference. In a world of brown, there sat a beacon of life. A white sign stood tall next to the road, stark against its dingy surroundings. On it was beautifully scripted letters in black and gold.

Miss Camille's Home for Wayward Children

The sign was lovely unto itself like no weather had ever worn it, but the truly odd thing was at the base of the sign. A tuft of lush green grass surrounded the posts holding it up. The greenery only seemed to be gathered in that spot and nowhere else.

As we got closer, tiny stalks raised up from the grass. They were moving like an animal slowly raising its head. At first, I thought my eyes might be deceiving me. One blink and they would go away. A trick of the sunlight maybe. The closer we got, however, the more real they became. When we were almost on top of the sign, the stalks opened their heads, and sunflowers bloomed big and yellow from each one.

It was unlike anything I'd ever seen. Flowers blooming from nothing in a matter of seconds, and timed exactly at our arrival. There was nothing I could say. My mouth hung open like carp on a line. I wondered what in heaven I got myself into.

In the end, I didn't need to ask. When I turned my disbelieving face to Camille, she was already beaming at me. Had she anticipated this? Had she caused it? Regardless, she seemed unmoved and entertained by my ignorance.

"I told you, young Galahad," she said with a knowing grin. "I'm in the witchin' business."

CHAPTER SIX

I don't know what I'd expected as far as houses went, but the ramshackle building wasn't at all what I'd pictured. With the flamboyant clothes and seemingly magical sign, any sort of house would have been appropriate in my mind. Something like a sultan's palace or maybe an elaborate estate was in order. Perhaps something made of candy and buttercream and peppermint sticks. But the two-story shack of a home at the end of the lane looked likely to fall over at any moment.

Polly had woken at that point and stood up to look over my shoulder. Her eyes were even wider than mine. We gawked at the place that looked to fall over in the next hard wind with understandable confusion. Polly and I didn't dare say anything, but it was as if Camille could read it in our expressions.

"Not everything is as appears, you two. What do they say? Don't judge a book by its cover? Well, don't judge this house by that either."

The property wasn't much to write home about. There was a decent bit of land around the house, but not enough to grow sellable crops. A small garden grew withering plants off to the north. Nearby was an even older looking barn. I worried leading Johnny Sanders inside such a structure as the roof might cave in on him at any moment.

Nevertheless, that was just what Camille instructed I do. For one reason or another, it was my job to do and do alone as she and Polly waited outside of the barn for me. It didn't occur to me that Camille was smiling like she knew something funny only to her. I was so shocked by all the events of the day, it was hard to notice anything that wasn't directly in front of me.

When I pushed the barn door aside, a whole other barn filled it. It was lavishly painted. Pristine wood stalls, crates of hay and oats. The roof looked positively watertight. I could smell the freshly dried staining on the wood. There was a new ladder leading up to a hayloft apartment. I spun in place, trying to take it all in. When I managed to turn back to the door, Polly was stepping cautiously inside.

She looked around with the same slack-jawed gape of wonder I did.

"What…what is this?"

"I said not to judge, didn't I?"

"You did, but how…?"

"You know, you keep forgettin' what business I am in, Nat. Must I remind you again and again? This will get irksome if I do."

I turned to face her. She had her arms crossed over her chest, leaning on the doorframe of the barn. For his part, Johnny looked annoyed at all of us. He just wanted oats.

"You can't be a witch. Witches ain't real."

"Oh no? Well, I will give you this much, witches ain't what people think. In fact, just about everyone has a little witch in them. We all possess the potential for great things. The woman who can suddenly lift far more than possible to save her children. The man who runs through bullets in war to save his friend. Most just never use it. Most don't know they can."

"But…but…how can you do this?"

"I'd love to tell you, but this is not my magic."

"Whose is it then?"

"Oh, you'll meet her. She's far better than me. You'll see."

"But why? Why have the outside of the barn look so bad? Why not just have the whole thing look this way?"

"Have you seen the world as it is of late? People have less than ever. There's dust everywhere, choking the crops and the people alike. The last thing we need is for them to start askin' why we have so much more. That gets people jealous. There is nothin' in this world more dangerous than desperate people possessed with the green-eyed monster."

"But, they already think you're witches. They think you turned a man into a mule," I protested. "Wouldn't they be too afraid…"

"Yes, but it wasn't someone they missed, was it? He was a pest. In the end, they didn't mind thinking I'd turned him into a mule. Got rid of him, and it helped me spread the idea to not mess with me or my kids. They are fine fearing us from a distance as long as we don't got more than them. That's when fear turns to anger. You get a group riled enough, the next step is violence no matter how scared they are."

I hadn't noticed, but while Camille and I were talking, Polly had led Johnny

Sanders to a stall and removed his bit. She pet his muzzle and leaned into his bulk for comfort.

"Do you scare her?" I asked Camille.

She nodded her head while watching Polly hug the animal.

"Probably. But based on her face when I mentioned him, I guarantee her daddy scares her more."

When we left the barn, both Polly and I had to take a few turns jumping in and out of the building, comparing the differences. Somehow, it helped solidify the thing in our minds. Camille waited patiently for us to finish before she continued with her tour of the bizarre home for wayward children.

We passed between a sparse garden and an empty parcel of land. It wouldn't have seemed peculiar at all if there hadn't been a solitary water spigot standing in the middle unattached to anything. I fixated on it for a moment. There was no crank or anything to pump to pull water up from a well. There wasn't even a base to it. Just a lonely faucet with a bucket nearby.

"Ah, I see you found our windmill," said Camille as followed my gaze.

"Windmill?"

"Yes, it does us the courtesy of pumping water and giving us energy."

"I don't see a windmill," I protested.

"You aren't looking correctly, Nat. You have to train your eyes to see beyond what's right in front of you. Look at it crooked. Try again."

I stared for a good long while. Nothing appeared to me. I squinted at the area where the windmill would be. All I could see was the pasture and trees beyond. My effort took so much of my focus, I didn't notice Polly sidling up next to me until she clapped me on the shoulder. When I spun to face her, she pointed up in the sky with a beautiful smile on her face.

There was a minute where I felt extremely embarrassed. I still saw nothing, merely wisps of white cotton in a clear blue sky. Then, there was a flash. Something too odd to explain in proper words. Another flash came right after. Then another and another. They were moving in rhythmic beats like something spinning. When I stopped looking directly at the sky and let my eyes daze away, I saw the movement of a windmill blade. One blade after another reflecting the sunlight at me. My body twitched, and I stared harder at where I'd seen the motion to get a fuller picture.

As soon as I caught it in my vision again, the entire thing appeared before me. I gasped it was so sudden and amazing. It was a fine windmill with white blades gently turning in the wind. Slow, and calming in a rhythm that only it knew. I listened hard, hearing the tiny picking noises of the gears inside turning. After I saw it, all I could think about how was it was possible I hadn't seen it before. When I looked over to Polly, she wore the same astonished face I did.

"There you go. You're getting it. Try the garden now," said Camille gesturing to the garden.

Polly and I turned our attention to the scraggly garden next to the house. At first, it looked like an amateur's attempt at a vegetable garden. There were some bean sprouts doing all right, and one tomato plant seemed to be producing a few small bulbs. Nothing spectacular. Most looked untended to, baked in the sun without enough water. Polly and I would have probably looked similar had we spent any more time by that post.

The thing of it was as soon as we looked at it crooked, the meager garden transformed into an oasis of plants. Tomato plants, bean, okra, corn, onions, everything one could want in a Texas garden. It was easier to see it now that I knew how to. Kind of like crossing your eyes and looking beyond.

My mouth must have been hanging open. Camille chuckled at me once again.

"I told you. We keep our bounty to ourselves. Most folks don't know to look this way. It's best to not tempt anyone. Keeps rabbits out of here too. Come on now, I'll take you inside."

There was nothing to do but follow her. I couldn't find the words, and Polly seemed to have none as it was. She reached out and took my hand in hers. Her thin fingers curled around my rough ones and squeezed harder than a girl her size ought.

"It's okay, Poll. I think this is a good place. I'll be right here if it ain't."

The house was the same as the barn; a ramshackle mess on the outside but pristine on the inside. Somehow it felt bigger too. Each room was larger than the outside perimeter allowed. The floors had new wood and plush carpets throughout. The urge to remove my boots and dig my toes in the fabric of the rugs had to be held in check. Every window had a curtain, and every door had antique handles. There were photos and paintings, honest to goodness paintings, on the wall. When we walked in, it smelled of chamomile and flowers.

"Alright now. Welcome to my home. This way is the kitchen. That's where Jacob will be. I'll introduce you."

We turned a corner that opened to a large kitchen, complete with all the amenities my Mamaw's kitchen never had. There were more cabinets than I could count, a deep sink, and a real stove with four drawers and a cooktop. Something sweet was baking somewhere, or perhaps that was the way this room always smelled.

While I was marveling at the kitchen, Polly honed in on a boy sitting at a small table next to the window. He couldn't have been more than six and wore a vibrant blue shirt with denim overalls. Before him on the table, was a chess set. He had similar coloring as Camille. When he looked up at me, he slowly moved the white knight chess piece forward and to the left.

"Hello?" I asked unsurely.

The boy waved with a big smile.

"He don't talk much. Well, he don't talk at all. This is Jacob. Jacob, this is Nat and Polly. They are going to be staying here with us for a while."

Jacob moved the white bishop across the board until it was right next to the white knight. When they were together, he nodded at Camille.

"Is that so? Well, I figured you would," she said to him.

"Did he say something?" I asked her.

"He said he knew you were coming."

"How do you know?"

"You'll figure it out as you go, but it's not big surprise. Jacob knows just about everything before it happens," she said and patted the boy on the arm.

Camille led us into the next room. I was hot on her heels while Polly lagged behind a bit to study Jacob's chess board.

"Is he your son," I asked.

"What a nosey question," said Camille without the slightest hint of irritation.

"My apologies. I ain't normally this forward, ma'am. This place got me a little thrown off."

"No problem whatsoever. I like some honesty. Polly dear, please catch up," Camille said beckoning to Polly from the next room. When the girl had caught up with us, she continued. "Jacob is not my son by birth, no. All the children who come to me for help feel like mine after a time. He's been with me the longest."

"How many others live here right now?" I asked.

"Well, there's Jacob, Crow, and Nan. Crow won't be around today, but you'll be meeting him soon enough, I reckon. I'm taking you down to see Nan now.

She's going to be so happy to meet you."

"Why do you do this?" I blurted out.

"Do what?"

"Why do you take in children? Why did you bring us here?"

Camille turned and leaned down a bit to level her eyes with mine.

"Like I said, I do value some honesty. It's a very useful thing, candor. There is a difference between honesty and rudeness. I appreciate your anxiety at present, Galahad, but I'm what you call a gift horse at the moment. Best not to go checkin' my teeth."

Not much to do but bow and nod my head. If anything she was right. No one made her help us. If things here went cross, I'd get Polly and run. Vigilance would be needed, but for now, I had to be grateful.

We made our way through the various rooms. Past a parlor done up like a pink, Victorian painting and a dining room with a table set for at least twelve people. It had a genuine crystal chandelier that threw bits of light all over the walls. I tried to track where we were and what turns would lead us back to the kitchen, but this place was a maze.

I wasn't ready for the door that led to the basement stairs. It was painted gold with a red, crystal doorknob. No, not painted gold. It looked like it was fashioned all over in gold leaf. There was no paint texture to it all. I had a sudden urge to touch it, to see if it was real, but that was quickly followed by the fear of ruining such a thing with my ugly hands. They hadn't been properly cut and groomed in a longer time than I cared to admit. Luckily, Camille did the honors for us and ventured down the stairs by the light of flame sconces.

The basement was like nothing I'd ever seen. Foreign-looking rugs covered the baseboards. One was stacked on top of another and another so no wood could be seen anywhere, just levels and levels of carpet. Our footsteps muffled as we walked on it. Lantern light gave the wide room a comforting glow since there were no windows to help. There was a small bed tucked in the corner with a plush mattress and at least a dozen pillows. It might have been comfortable if you didn't mind caves.

Nan was off in another corner. She was an old woman, her dark skin plum-colored in the shadows. The dress she wore looked like a hodgepodge of curtains thrown over and around her, and her wooly, white hair was pulled loosely into a wrap. She sat before an easel with a canvas on it. The painting she worked at looked like a portrait. A hazy silhouette of a face stared back at her.

There were lots of canvases strewn about the same way. Portraits of people. All ages and all genders. The one thing that made them the same was the way they were painted. Their skin appeared dim like there were only partly there. Like looking a person through frosted glass. The eyes were completely gone, giving a sense of nothingness where their gaze would have been. I stood in a room with dozens of ghostly faces staring black eyes back at me.

When Nan turned around, she was all smiles. She was missing several teeth, and the ones that were there didn't seem to be fairing too well. It was a warm enough greeting, but I still trembled with the paintings all around. It felt like they were watching me.

"Ah, the new ones. Jacob told me to expect you," said Nan in a gentle voice.

"He *told* you?" I asked.

"Yes, of course. This must be Nat. Very lovely to meet you," Nan said extending her hand to me.

I hadn't noticed until that moment, but she was wearing very fine kid-skin gloves. When I looked just past her and beyond the easel, there were lots of pairs of gloves. Work gloves, satin gloves, fine gloves, and cotton gloves. They hung in all manner of colors around the room the way a butcher might hang his cuts for the day.

The whole place was odd, and I wanted to ask about a hundred questions. Well, part of me did, and other part wanted to run screaming.

"Now now, son. I know you have questions, but there'll be time for that. Right now, if you shake my hand, I'll answer one of them before Camille escorts you to your separate rooms."

I reached out and shook her hand. It was boney under her gloves.

"There now. This is Polly, yes?"

Polly didn't hesitate the way I had. She shook Nan's hand right away. Camille merely stood aside and let the show play out before her.

"So, I get to ask one question then?" I asked cautiously.

"That was the deal. Ask away, young Nat. Only one right now. I'm an old lady and need my beauty rest. The others will wait until later."

There were so many questions to ask. I looked around the strange room and pondered which one I needed to know that moment. Which one would eat away at my insides if I didn't know right then? I picked the most frightening thing in the room.

"The portraits," I blurted out. "Those pictures you're painting. Why do they look like that? Who are those people?"

Nan's smile grew so wide it barely left any room on her face for anything else. She reached down by her feet and retrieved a canvas with the portrait of a ghostly soldier.

"This is the portrait of Private Benjamin Stokes," she said, gesturing to his face.

Polly and I stared at the portrait as if waiting for there to be more. At first, there wasn't anything more, and I worried there wouldn't be an explanation for it at all. When I looked over to Camille for help, she put up her hand as if telling me to wait.

"He passed during the great war. No one even found his body."

"Why are you paintin' his portrait? Why do you paint any of these?" I asked, losing my patience with the whole show.

"Because dear boy, he's dead. They're all dead."

Nan started pointing to each picture in kind.

"She's dead, he's dead, and that one? Oh, he's definitely dead."

"I…I don't understand."

"I paint their ghosts. Dead folks come to me because they want to be remembered. They can't pass on if no one remembers what they look like. It can be so easy to be forgotten."

"You…you paint their ghosts?"

"Yes. It makes them feel better," she said as plainly as if she were informing me it was Tuesday. "They can rest easier when someone's got their picture. Somewhere they are remembered, if only in a painting."

My head swiveled around the room. Solemn, ghostly faces stared back at me. Without eyes to focus, they all seemed to be staring right at me no matter where I moved or where I looked. Each one had a longing in its face, a deep sense of sorrow like someone who lost something valuable. Dead people, the lot of them. I was looking at dead people.

Shivery tingles infected me. It made the fleshy bits around my spine jump and twitch. I made a good show of keeping my hands and legs steady, but every part of my body was screaming for me to run for my life.

I looked to Polly to see if she was as frightened as I was. The thing of it was, she stood there smiling. Twirling in a circle, Polly gazed from one portrait to the next and beamed at them like it was a room full of treasures. Like they were pictures of candy and dolls. Where I saw horror, what did she see? Peace and beauty? How could one tell with a girl who refused to speak?

I stood there, a man alone in a house full of loons.

CHAPTER SEVEN

Our rooms were not at all what I expected. After the lavishness in the rest of the house and the crazy encounter with Nan, I feared what oddities might be waiting for me. Beds that devoured you in your sleep. Gargoyles in the dresser. Wriggling things that lived under the bed.

When Camille opened the door, the strangest thing greeted me. I couldn't imagine any other sight to be that surprising.

The room was normal; sparse to be sure but normal. There was a bed, a washbasin, a chest of drawers, and a bookshelf. Some light blue curtains hung over the windows that matched the quilt on the bed, but that was it. Even the quilt was bland. It bore no pattern, not even the smallest variance in the stitching. Everything stood out as starkly plain. No terrifying paintings, or strange photographs. No Dracula in the corner. There wasn't even a rug.

Polly's room was directly across the hall. Her room looked exactly the same as mine but with yellow curtains and a yellow quilt. Had it not been a cheered by the light pouring in through the window, the thought of prison cells would have come to mind.

Camille looked joyfully at the matching looks on our faces.

"So sorry it's not up to your standards, my lord and lady," Camille retorted with an exaggerated bow.

"It ain't that," I said, not wanting to sound ungrateful. "It's just the rest of the house is so…well…odd. I think we were 'specting…"

"Ghosts in the mirrors? Goblins hangin' from chandeliers?"

"Well, somethin' along those lines."

"This here is your room," she said putting a hand on my shoulder. "I ain't one to tell you how your room should look. The rest of the house takes on the personalities of the folks livin' in it. This is no different. You two got a clean slate here. It will decorate as you choose."

I didn't understand her meaning, and at that point, I was too tired to even try. My body moved forward without my mind telling it to, just going through the motions of keeping me alive. The idea of fresh water and maybe some clean clothes was heaven.

After Camille left us to our rooms, I washed my face in the basin. The water was cold like it hadn't been sitting in a Texas afternoon. I nearly groaned with happiness as I wet my neck and splashed it around my chest and under my arms. The last bath I took was probably a month previous, and it was in a stock tank at that. When staring down weeks of grit and rubble, the stench of manure around a stock tank was wonderful. This, however, was pure bliss.

The rags I was wearing were the next to go. When I searched the chest of drawers, I found clean clothes. To my utter surprise, they were boy's clothes. I retrieved a shirt and some britches. The shirt would do just fine and so would the britches even though they were a bit short on the legs. Given that Camille just met me, I wondered how she came by clothes so quickly. Jacob wouldn't have been able to fit into these. The shirt alone would swallow him. Had she been anticipating our arrival? Before today, I might have said that was a bunch of bull, but after coming to *Miss Camille's House for Wayward Children*, I didn't know anymore.

Polly came out when I knocked on her door. Her sack was gone, and in its place was a pale, yellow dress. What a difference a change of clothes made. The dirt and grime had been washed from her face, and her hair was wetted back. Her new dress was a little large around the chest but fit her well enough. Her skinny legs and knobby knees looked like a regular girl's in a dress like that. I hoped for her sake some good meals would help her fill out to a healthier size.

She appraised my appearance as well. Her large, hazel eyes looking from my pants to my face. Though she smiled a bit at the high hem of my pant legs, Polly gave me a nod of approval.

"That in your room too?" I asked pointing to her dress.

She nodded.

"How you suppose they got clothes fer us? We only just met today."

Polly shrugged.

"You want to go 'splorin' with me? As long as we stay away from that creepy cellar?"

Her face lit up, a smile from ear to ear. Polly grabbed my hand and dragged me down the hallway. Apparently, that's what she'd been wanting to do as well.

We found our way back to the kitchen where Jacob still sat. He waved at us enthusiastically from his seat by the chess board but wouldn't get up. Across the kitchen was a larger, breakfast table. On it sat a large bowl full to the brim with fruit. Apples, oranges, and even bananas. Before I registered what I was doing, I had walked over to the table and snatched a banana. Polly did the same with a ruby red apple.

No one stopped us, so we went ahead and ate the fruit, as much as we could stomach. I figured if this really was our home now, we could partake of food left out in the open. By the time we were done eating, and my belly was full, I realized I had no idea where to go from there. This was a maze of a house. We were lucky to have found the kitchen at all. I spun around in a circle. There were three different exits to the kitchen. It was hard to tell which way to go.

"Which way should we go," I asked addressing Jacob. "If we wanted to explore a bit, I mean."

Jacob pointed through a hallway just behind us.

"You wanna come with us?" I asked.

He shook his head no but smiled all the same. I thanked him and led Polly out of the kitchen. The next room was painted all red. Fine, elegant designs in white were drawn over and over again on the walls. They were perfectly spaced like a machine had printed it over and over again. Polly thought it was particularly lovely. She got close to the wall and ran her small finger along the edge of the filigree. The design was raised from the wall and fine to the touch.

The whole room looked like some sort of parlor where fancy folks might sit and discuss…well…what every fancy folks talked about, but I got chills just walking into it. Suddenly my shirt wasn't enough to keep me warm. The little hairs on my arms stood at attention. The temperature in this room varied so drastically from the others Polly left the wall and leaned into me, goose bumps covering her arms.

We moved closer inside. Overstuffed chairs made of velvet, or something like it, was in every corner. Touching them felt like petting a warm peach. Small corner tables had fine paintings on the top of fancy women having picnics. A tea set in fine china with little rabbits painted on it sat empty and waiting for no one on the middle table. I looked up to see the perfectly rounded wooden ceiling and bumped into the lamp next to me. It jingled with fringe and little jewels.

In the center was a fireplace with two plush chairs on either side. To my utter surprise, a fire roared there behind a screen. Just above the fireplace, a deer's head was mounted. He was a decent-sized buck on a plaque of fine rosewood.

His regal eyes stared emptily ahead. That was, until they didn't. In a flash, they changed their direction to look directly down at me. I jumped and made to call out, but as soon as I opened my mouth, he looked away.

"Poll, did you see…?"

When I looked at her, she was engrossed in a painting behind us. It was a snowy landscape with a cabin among the trees. A few deer grazed in the woods in the background. I looked back at the buck, but he seemed unmoved. Surely, he hadn't looked down at me. His eyes were glass like any other mounted creature, or so I told myself.

The next room was a library and a blissful relief. I stepped into the library and felt lighter than air. This room was vast with pillows and blankets thrown around in corners. Huge windows went from the floor to the ceiling with padded, window box benches under each one. The library was bright and airy, and it smelled of old books and dried ink. Every corner seemed a wonderful place to rest and drift away for a while.

While I walked into the room in awe, Polly ran past me with excitement. She twirled in place, smiling up to the high ceilings. I watched her as she walked up and down the bookshelves, running her hand along the spines. I didn't know how many books there were in the world, but I wagered most of them rested here in this library. Nothing I'd seen could compare.

There was a particularly handsome volume bound in blue leather sitting on the shelf. Polly was at my side in an instant as I pulled the book from the shelf. It had a clasp on it made of silver. It creaked as I opened the book and peered inside.

The pages were blank.

Nothing could have shocked me more at that moment. Not even the blandness of my strange room. As I flipped through the pages, I stared in wonder as all of them before me were blank. No title. No pictures. Nothing. Just paper fluttering against my fingers, creating its own small breeze against my face.

"Who would keep a book with nothing in it?" I asked, turning to Polly.

She shrugged, and I started pulling out more books and looking through them. I must have pulled a half a dozen off the shelf, and not a one had anything written on it at all.

"They ain't books per se," said a croaky voice behind us.

We spun around to find Nan in all her layers of fabric entering the library through an alternate door. She wore green, satin gloves that ran all the way up to her elbows so pristine they could have been recently bought from the store. Nan smiled at us as she used an old cane to hobble our way.

"What are they if they ain't book?" I asked.

"Placeholders. They are placeholders for books. They hold a spot in the world for books too special to stay put for long."

"What's that mean?"

"See. Look here," Nan said as she took a small, yellow book from the shelf.

She held the book out for us to see. When she opened the cover, words began to appear where the title page should have been.

The Ancient Practice of Illusion

Nan grinned at our befuddled faces. The more pages she turned, the more words appeared. I was a slow reader, but I did pick up some of the words. They mainly spoke of tricks of the eye. The ease of misdirection. Hiding objects in between the air and eyes.

Polly turned to the bookcase and grabbed a book the color of rusted metal. I watched her chest rise and fall with a deep breath as she contemplated the empty cover. When she opened it, nothing happened. Still, the blank pages that were always there.

"Close your eyes, child. Let your gut tell you," whispered Nan.

Polly shut her eyes, holding the book shut like a holy thing. Such reference in that grip. We watched her takes several deep and measured breaths again. When her brow pinched with concentration, Nan reached over and rubbed it until it smoothed. Finally, Polly opened her eyes and turned her book to the title page. The title filled with ink just as it did with Nan's book.

Teleportation: Twelve Ways to Move Through Space

"Ahhhh, that's a good one. I read it myself many years ago. It hasn't showed up in a while though. No one seems to call it. Good to see it again."

I gazed at the book in wonderment. Polly's mouth hung open in a wide O of surprise. She looked up into Nan's old eyes, and whispered, "Thank you."

Polly left us without even a pause, not even an explanation as to why she chose that moment to start speaking. She just ran to the nearest window bench seat and plopped down with her new book. I reckoned she must have been starved for reading, or maybe it was the excitement of having a book just appear to you and only you.

I reached for my blue volume I'd dropped on the floor. There was a giddy expectation when I opened it. I closed my eyes and concentrated the way Polly had and wondered what strange volume would reveal itself to me. When I opened the cover, it still sat the same in my hands. Blank and wordless.

"I don't get it," I said to Nan.

"Sometimes it takes time," she replied simply.

"What does that mean? Why did Polly's show up?"

"Don't worry, child. You ain't old enough yet to block the words. It's full grown people with no imagination who block them out completely. That's not you, not yet. Even then, not everyone finds their book right off. It will come when you're ready."

None of it made any sense, but nothing that day made any sense either. Fighting for reason in my mind hurt, and questions raced through so fast I couldn't stop any long enough to ask, so I opted to surrender things to the way they were presented for the time being. In an effort to ease my headache, I would jot the questions down and revisit them another time.

It was about that time I saw a framed picture on the bookshelf a level above my head. The frame itself was a pretty thing, all gilded in silver, but it was the subject in the picture that took my attention. There were two people, a boy and a girl, in the photograph. Both were so peculiar-looking I couldn't help but stare. They had fair skin and had hair so blond, it was nearly white. There was no doubt they were related they looked so much alike. The two odd creatures stood looking at the camera holding hands. Behind them were rows and rows of corn.

"Who's that?" I asked Nan, pointing to the photograph.

"Oh, those are the Frost twins."

"The Frost twins?"

"Yes. David and Delphia Frost. They lived here for a piece. Lovely children. I miss them so much, especially since the house has been so empty. So lovely. You'd be hard pressed to find two gentler people in the world."

"Where did they go? What happened to them?" I asked.

"That's not a story to tell right now. Too much on your first day, I'm afraid."

"But, I want to know," I protested.

"Someday soon. I promise you."

Nan patted my shoulder gently, and I relented. It wasn't the gesture that silenced me any more than it was her promise to tell me in the future. When I studied the photograph a bit further, I noticed what the girl was wearing. Delphia Frost was wearing a pale dress in the picture. The photograph had no color, so it was impossible to tell for sure, but I wagered my life that dress was a light yellow color. It looked exactly like the one Polly was wearing.

CHAPTER EIGHT

When Camille said she was going to town a few days later, I jumped at the chance to go along for the ride. It wasn't that anyone in the house was unkind. Everyone had been more than polite to us, and the food was better than I'd had in ages. Smoked meats and fresh vegetables every day. There was even a hidden orchard behind the line of trees. Bananas came from somewhere, but Camille never said where.

It was the strangeness of the place that set my teeth on edge. Everything felt alive, even down to the furniture. After my frustrating ordeal in the library, the bookshelf in my room began filling up with novels. A few I had read myself but new ones popped up as well. They appeared out of nowhere in twos and threes.

At first, I reckoned it was Camille sneaking them in, hoping to make me feel at home. I didn't know how she could, but it was my only theory. However, it happened anytime I was away, even when we were all together. I joined everyone for breakfast in the kitchen, and when I'd return, there were two new books waiting for me. They were good books, ones I wanted to read, but there was no explanation for them.

That was a good description for the entire house really. Everything was odd but not in a bad way. We were treated well and fed well. I had full run of the house, but I couldn't handle exploring for long. Every time I did, something odd would happen, and I'd go back to my room. Just when I thought I had mapped a hallway, another door would appear. How could a person rest their feet on solid ground if the ground never stayed solid?

Once, I found a room that seemed really pretty at first, all bright with sunflowers growing in bunches on the floor. A small, carpeted pathway allowed me to move around the flowers without disturbing them. Some were nearly shoulder high to me.

It wasn't until the buzzing started that my hair stood on end. Bees dropped down slowly enough at first like dark, floating raindrops hovering around my head. I held my breath. Someone had once told me bees were attracted to your breath and fear. Fear was the other thing they liked, but I didn't know how to control that.

One of them flew right at eye level to me, staring me down as if bees could do such a thing. I held my breath and tried to swallow hard against the urge to run. Without prompt, he flew straight into my forehead. With a thud, he bounced off and flew away. No damage, no sting, but I couldn't help feeling it was a warning.

Off to the left was a glass jar fixed to the wall. It had the weirdest yellow mess oozing down it, like amber molasses…or…honey. A din of buzzing got louder as I looked up at the ceiling, and I instantly regretted walking into that room at all. The jar followed the crease of the corner until it smacked straight into the largest beehive I'd ever seen. Millions of angry posy pokers covered the entire ceiling of the strange room. Their hive left no room for paint or paper to be seen.

My heart pounded for all it was worth, and I ran away from the sound of a million angry bees hot on my tail. I shut the door behind me and heard a dozen little bodies smack into it behind me.

Never had I felt like such a coward. It wasn't a part of my character I liked seeing. It was then I decided I wouldn't explore any further in the house alone. If this was how Camille got her honey, I didn't want to know how the bananas showed up.

Any time I asked Camille for work to do, she'd shrug me off. She gave excuses for not having anything or that I needed to settle in. Truth was my mind was running in circles, and in the morning she said she was going into town, I practically leapt at the chance to go with her. Anything to go somewhere normal.

The wagon pulled up to the sign, and yet again, the sunflowers bloomed as we neared. I watched them as we rode past. The blooms didn't wilt, more like folded in on themselves and tucked back into their grass around them. Sunflowers were pretty when there were no bees around.

"Do they always do that?" I asked. "The flowers, I mean."

"Most of the time. As long as everything is good and the people passin' are friendly."

Camille eyed me across the bench seat.

"You doing alright there, Nat? How are you adjustin' to the new home?"

"It was very kindly of you to take me in," I said without looking up at her.

"That's true, but you didn't answer me proper."

"I don't want to seem ungrateful."

"You won't. I promise."

"Well, pardon my sayin' so, Miss Camille, but I just don't know what to think. Everything's odd, Jacob never seems to leave his table, he doesn't talk, and I can't go anywhere near Nan's room."

"Why not? She didn't do something ugly, did she?"

"No, Nan's nice to me. It's just all so different and…well…different."

"I see," Camille said with a snicker. "You don't like it."

"No, it's not that. I just…don't understand it. I can't find where I fit."

"Polly seems to like it," she added.

"Yes, she spends all day reading her book. None of the books work for me like that."

"I thought you had a bookcase of them in your room?"

"Those aren't the magic books. Those are novels," I said with a sigh.

"Funny, I thought novels were magic books," she said with a snicker. "Look here Nat, you ain't found your place yet. The important word there is *yet*. I think you'll like it soon enough. If not, you are welcome to go as you like. I won't ever keep a person here that don't want it."

"I think…I think if I could…work, that might help. Bein' busy suits me. When I'm not, I just sit around mullin' things over and makin' myself nuts."

"Fair enough, young Galahad. Fair enough indeed. I'll put you to work, but don't you work too hard now and forget to check in with your magic books. They are important. More important in my opinion."

"Yes, ma'am."

As we entered the town proper, it was nearly deserted. The few people around twitched and bolted like jackrabbits into the nearest buildings as we came their way. Agitation filled in the spaces between the breeze and the smell of manure. Even Johnny Sanders flipped his ears back and forth like something was off.

Camille's normally jovial face drew taught and concerned. All the hairs on my neck stood at attention as though I were a tomcat in a fight. The battle hadn't come yet, but I could smell it, whatever it was.

"What's going on?"

"Fear, a lot of it," said Camille.

"I thought you said it was good for the townsfolk to be a little afraid of us."

"A little afraid yes, but this ain't a little. This is different. Besides, I can't catch wind of what they're afraid of. Might not be us directly. Might be somethin' else."

We hitched Johnny Sanders and the wagon behind the general store. Camille said it made it easier to load supplies, but I figured it also hid the wagon from looky-loos on the street. There was no mistaking *her* wagon. Something had everyone agitated. Better not to dangle a steak in front of a hungry dog.

Norman Jackson nearly jumped out of his skin when the bell jingled to announce our arrival. He didn't calm much when he saw it was Camille who entered.

"Jehoshaphat, Camille. You scared me half to death," said Norman.

"I can see that. What's goin' on, Norman?"

"You should go. You and the boy should go. Really."

"Well, we ain't doin' that. I'm here to pick up my order. You got it or not?"

Norman shuffled behind the counter, a jittering June bug in man's clothes. When he opened the door to the back storeroom, he motioned us inside. Camille and I obliged him, and he shut the door behind my back.

"The Elder Jones is on a tear, Camille. He knows someone took his girl from off the post. Been walkin' up and down the square, questionin' folks. I didn't give you up, but my guess is someone else did. The man's on a tear for you."

"Which Elder Jones is this now? There are what...five of 'em?" asked Camille with an aloof shrug.

"Don't joke about this, Camille. I like you. You're a nice lady. I don't want you to get hurt, but I told you not to take that white girl."

"Norman, you are a prince among swine. Truly a gentleman. You and Galahad load these things up 'round back. I'll lead Johnny Sanders to meet ya. We'll get out of here, so you don't get in trouble, okay?"

He nodded and led me to a pile of goods in the corner of the storeroom. Camille disappeared back into the store. The door's jingle let us know when she'd left out of the front. It took several trips, but we managed to carry everything out back and load the wagon in record time. Norman was still twitching when Camille paid for her purchases.

"Norman, did I not specifically tell you I wished to know when Miss

Lavendou arrived in the city proper?" said a loud, deep voice from the street behind us.

I nearly jumped a foot in the air. We all turned to see the man I knew to be Polly's father striding toward us slowly. He had a long stride with his hands folded behind his back. Norman took three steps away, and I reached for the pistol tucked in the back of my pants. Camille calmly reached out a hand to stop me. I still had no bullets, but he didn't know that.

"Elder Jones, lovely day isn't it? I hear you've been looking for me."

As the man in the black suit strode up to her, he smiled down into her grinning face. He was even taller in person; perhaps two heads taller than Camille. She didn't move a muscle. Not even a twitch.

"I did not know until quite recently that my quest for my daughter would lead me to you, Miss Lavendou. However, friends around here have informed me as much. Can't say it surprises me. You have taken her to your home and are holding her there against her will. I require her return. Quickly and quietly would be my preference, but I can play any hand you wish."

His voice sounded like honey, but the malice made his words a bitter thing. Camille squared off against the man. It wasn't a noticeable gesture if you weren't standing right next to her. Her feet parted just enough to be under her hips, evening out her weight on the ground. Each hand found its place on her hips, not balled into fists but ready all the same. She narrowed her eyes in the direction of the tall adversary.

"Well, that is a very interesting assessment of our current predicament. I have to say it ain't the truth of the matter. Your daughter? She went along only after I invited her. She is not at my home against her will, and she is free to go at any time as long as she wants to."

"But you do have her? My daughter?"

"It seems to me, and please do tell me if I'm wrong, you threw that girl away. I found the child half-starved and chained to a post. Most people wouldn't do that sort of thing to a dog, let alone a daughter."

Elder Jones's smile vanished, but Camille's didn't. She was just getting warmed up.

"She was paying her penance. It was none of your affair," he said sternly.

"Her penance? Huh, that's a funny thing. What would be your penance if she died like that? Or worse? Well, whatever you call it, it's over now. You threw that child away, and I took her in with her permission."

"What about my permission?" he growled. "You didn't have that. She is a child. Sheriff Barnesby will raid that hovel you call home if I give him the go ahead. Just you watch and see."

"Hmmmmm. I don't think that's happenin'. Sheriff Barnesby might be in your back pocket, but he reports to Amarillo. The man in charge there is a lovely fellow by the name Percy Armstrong. You remember him, don't you? One of Nan's boys. Grew up in that very same *hovel* your daughter is in right now. He's very sympathetic to our cause as I'm sure you know."

"What sort of cause is there to support kidnapping children?"

"Oh dear sir, I don't kidnap anyone. None of us do. The lawful definition of kidnappin' is to take someone illegally against their will violently or by fraud. I assure you I did none of those things. Just ask Nat over here. The boy can bear witness. He came with me the same time as Poll. Tell us, Nat, did I force you to come with me to participate in the devil's work?"

The large man turned his glare to me, and I gripped the pistol's handle harder behind my back. It wasn't the time back down, so I set my eyes on him.

"No, Miss Camille. You didn't," I said through grinding teeth.

"Did I in any way apply fraud to lure you to my den of evil?"

"No, Miss Camille."

"You were there with Polly when she came with me. Did you witness me forcefully drag her or conduct myself fraudulently to get her to come with us?"

"No, ma'am. She came with you happily because it was a might bit better than going back to this sorry excuse of a man," I said in the deepest voice I could muster.

"You little shit," said Elder Jones as he turned on me with white rage in his eyes.

One flip of Camille's hand stopped him.

"This here argument over the law is between you and me, sir. Do not threaten that boy."

The Elder turned to her as she requested. He moved in close, too close for Camille's comfort. She took a step backwards, and one hand went to her belt. I hadn't noticed until she made the motion, but on her wide, leather belt sat a black pouch. With a quick hand motion, she flipped the lid of the pouch open and shoved her hand inside. Elder Jones stopped in tracks; the first traces of fear flashed in his eyes. It was an odd look on his face, but whatever was in Camille's pouch brought it out.

"Give me my daughter back," he spat at her.

"You threw her away, Joseph. You don't scare me none. Not even a little. The law is on my side. She's old enough to decide, and you threw her away like garbage."

"She is a witch…a devil," he said, practically foaming at the mouth like an animal.

"Then she'll be in marvelous company," retorted Camille with venom in her grin.

For every man in that square bit of alley, the tension was horrible. The heat was getting to me, and sweat rolled off my arms and down my fidgety hands. Norman kept inching toward his store, hands already slightly up as if surrendering before the fact. Even Elder Jones was tense all over, his mouth set in a hard line. Camille, on the other hand, looked as though she were about to stroll through a meadow on an autumn evening. She smiled wide at him, showing all her teeth the way a cat might.

I could have sworn that would have tipped the man over the edge. Camille was a colored woman living in a white man's world after all. Whomever this man really was, it was obvious there was a good bit of money and power behind him. Yet when he stood toe to toe with her, he was the first to flinch. Elder Jones took a few steps back, and Camille retrieved her hand from the pouch on her belt. The standoff was at an end, at least for the time being.

"This trespass will not go unnoticed, Miss Lavendou. You have overstepped your place by taking my daughter."

"I took no one. She came with me as I've said before. Perhaps if you treated your women with an ounce of respect, they wouldn't keep running away on you," she snapped.

"I will personally see to your damnation."

"I do reckon that's God's job, Joseph. Or did you forget you two are not one and the same?"

He gave her one last, dark glare before he turned on his heel and stormed away. Norman had ducked back into his store by the time we made it to the wagon. My teeth positively chattered when I pulled myself up on the bench seat next to her. We didn't say a word to one another as Johnny Sanders lurched forward, steering us out of the alley and onto the street.

The town was ghostly quiet again. No one, not even Elder Jones, graced us with their presence. An eerie silence moved through the square like a slow wake before us. It lingered among the streets long after we left.

"What was that?" I asked when we finally had the buildings of Tanglewood behind us.

"That terrible excuse for a man was Elder Joseph Jones. Otherwise known as Polly's father. He's a violent zealot of the first order. Take enough wives, and a man thinks he's a god."

"You ain't afraid of him?"

"What do you think?" she asked with a smirk.

"Well, everyone else seems to be."

"Everyone else is beholden to him. Like I said, his commune of followers keep a lot of businesses running. They own quite a bit of land down here and quite a few bank notes on the farms."

"But you ain't afraid."

"Quickest way to get a bully to leave you alone is to show him you ain't afraid. He'll bluster a bit, but in the end, there's nothin' he can do. A bully is a bully no matter how old or what suit he wears."

I looked down at my hands. A question hung in the air I wanted to pluck, but I had asked something similar before, and Camille wasn't having any of it then.

"Why'd you do it? Why did you take in Polly? I mean, no one wants me, but you had to know who she was and who her daddy was. Why do it?"

Camille looked at me as though I should already know the answer like my question was a stupid one. My face flushed under her scrutiny.

"I did it the same reason you helped her, Galahad. She needed helpin'. You saw the same thing I did when I saw her. A poor girl needin' someone to protect her. I don't care who her daddy is, and I wouldn't take it back for anything in world."

Camille patted my knee playfully and socked me on the shoulder.

"Now, ask me a question that isn't so dumb. I do declare that was the worst question I've heard in five years. You need to come up with something better, or I will lose all respect for you."

She tussled my hair under my hat. I couldn't help but laugh back as I playfully pushed her off me. My smile was easy and welcomed after so much tension. The world was full of sounds again, the sweet songs of birds and crickets. Somewhere in the sky, a hawk screamed against a warm draft. It reminded me not everything revolved around our little story in a strange house.

"The law stuff. How'd you know all those big words fer things?"

"That's easy. A woman like me has to educate herself about her rights. Come on, you can do better than that."

"Okay okay. The pouch thing, what is that? What does he think you have in there?"

"Oh that," said Camille giggling to herself. "The folks 'round here think I have a deadly weapon in this here pouch."

I leaned over as she opened the pouch lid enough to show me inside. It was hard to know what to expect, but what I saw was not what one would expect a deadly weapon to look like. The pouch was filled with little, black balls. There were dozens of them, no bigger than a dime. I looked up at Camille for some sort of explanation.

"They think they're full of mosquitos," she said flipping the lid back on the pouch.

"Mosquitos?"

"Yes. The story goes if I throw these at a person, the balls burst and release thousands of mosquitos that do my bidding. They will swarm a man and devour him in minutes. Bones and all!"

My mouth hung open, remembering the beautiful room with the bees. I was so numb from trying to connect pieces together, I didn't notice that a gnat found himself inside my mouth. The sudden buzzing frightened me after the story of the mosquitos, and I flipped my wig trying to spit the thing out. By the time I composed myself, Camille had nearly fallen off the bench seat from laughing.

"That…that can't be true," I stammered. "That can't actually be a real thing, can it? I mean, it's one of your ruses, right? To scare people into leaving you alone, I mean. Like with Johnny Sanders?"

"Oh my dear Galahad, I'd love to tell you, but I won't. Not just yet. Not every moment is meant for explainin' things. Some are for laughing, and some are just for honey. Pickin' it to death tends to blow so much sparkle off of what's to come later."

CHAPTER NINE

After a hot day in town, the strangely cold study was an inviting idea. I couldn't find Polly anywhere, so after I helped Camille unload the supplies in the barn, the study was my next destination.

Sweat pooled around my neck, under my waistband, and beneath my arms. Those places were hot and damp while the rest of my body was itchy where the moisture had already dried. A change of clothes would be in order, but first I desperately wanted to cool off. Nothing harder than changing clothes when your body was salty and wet. It was like wrestling a cat in a sweater.

The study was blessedly empty. After all that had happened, the last thing I wanted was company. I needed alone time to contemplate everything. It was my chance to restore my wits in a sea of din. If nothing else, the study would be quiet and free from the strange.

I took the chair furthest from the fireplace and kicked my boots off in a corner. The coolness of the room enveloped me, turning the humid parts of my body cold and allowing them to breathe once again. The humidity of my feet turned icy, cooling the hot spots my boots left. I stretched out my arms and closed my eyes to gentle silence.

"This is so much better," I said to myself.

"Well, maybe for you," replied a voice from somewhere in the room.

Suddenly aware I wasn't alone, I sat upright and looked around the room. There appeared to be no one there. The room was empty save myself.

"I mean really. You must know how much you smell," said the voice again.

Upon hearing the voice a second time, I realized it was coming from above me. I followed it over to the fireplace and up to the mounted buck's head. To my disbelief, the head was looking directly down at me, an annoyed grimace on his face.

"I don't mind the sweat as much, but did you really have to take your shoes off? I mean, it's just rude," said the deer.

"I...I...I didn't know anyone was in here," I replied.

It was a weird thing replying to the dead remains of a deer mounted on the wall. Had I not already seen stranger in this place, I might have run away screaming.

"Well, of course, I'm in here. This is my room. How could you not notice me? I'm a fine specimen. Everyone says so," he said with an air of conceit.

"Yes, I see that. It's just that...I didn't expect you to be alive. You're the first talking head I've ever met."

"Oh, I doubt that. Talking heads are everywhere from what I understand. Besides, how would you know if you never asked any of them?"

"I reckon I wouldn't," I said shrugging.

"Precisely. Now, if you wouldn't mind replacing your shoes. Truly it is beginning to smell like an awful sort of bog in this room."

"My apologies."

I retrieved my boots while trying to wrap my brain around the idea I was speaking with a talking bust of a deer. A pompous one at that.

"Your name is Nat, I've heard," said the buck when I had slipped my boots back into place.

"Yep, that's me. What is your name?"

"Oh, I have no name. We deer don't need frivolous things like names. A completely mundane practice if you ask me. Naming things that is."

"Then what should I call you?"

"Buck, if you must."

"Your name is Buck?"

"No, I thought we went over that already. Really, do try to keep up. This is what other people like to call me, so if you must call me something, you may use it."

"I see."

"And I'm telling you, you won't find a better specimen than me to look upon. I've been around, and I have the finest antlers out there. Anyone will tell you so. They are perfectly spaced and proportioned, don't you agree?"

He seemed to want my opinion, so I took my time observing his antlers to prove my sincerity before speaking. Never had I been asked to judge the quality of a dead animal's antlers before, but far stranger things had happened that day, so I decided to play along to get along.

"I have to say, they are fine. Finer than any I've seen," I replied.

I'd never seen a deer smile, but I suppose that's what Buck tried to do. The edges of his lips curled upward ever so slightly. His eyes gleamed in the firelight.

"And my nose. The perfect proportion for my face. See how dashing it makes me look?"

"It is a perfect nose, I must admit," I said with a fake smile.

"And my eyes, oh, my eyes! Just the pinnacle of class."

For a brief moment, I wanted to say they were the pinnacle of glass. Surely they were made in a taxidermist's shop. Real deer eyes wouldn't still be around after an animal's death. In the end, I refrained and played along some more.

"Not even royalty could compare," I said.

"Yes, I know. They are lovely. Too lovely to waste on you, I'm afraid."

"What do you mean?"

"You are dismissed."

"From where?"

"My room of course," he said as though I were a moron. "Now that you have covered those smelly things, it's time for you to go. One shouldn't host strangers too long. It can wear a body out. I simply have had enough of you. Go now. Your little friend is out back. I dismissed her and her book earlier."

When presented with a terrible amount of bizarre things, a mind will eventually give up and comply. I threw my hands up in defeat, bade the talking deer head good afternoon, and found my way out to the back porch of the house.

Polly was there as Buck said, sitting in a porch swing and reading from her book. While the front of the house looked dilapidated for the viewing of any passing strangers, the back was luxurious. There was a large covered patio, flowers blooming in giant pots at every post. The wood of the patio was painted a creamy sort of white. Even the swing Polly sat in was white with a yellow and blue cushion. She looked like a picture curled up in a pink paisley dress, the sunlight just barely touching her feet.

"Hi there," I said.

"Hello," Polly responded.

Nothing she did would have surprised me more. What a day for surprises this had been. Polly had spoken very little to anyone since I found her in town that fateful day. Not so much as a whisper other than her small "thank you" to Nan in the library. Most of our talks had been achieved as they always had. I talked, and she shrugged.

Too many bizarre things. Just too many. I stopped dead in my tracks and searched her eyes for some sort of clue as to what changed that fact today.

"You. You are talking?"

"I can," she replied simply.

"Then why haven't you?"

"Didn't want to. Wasn't safe."

"But it's okay to talk now?"

She nodded and said, "I think it is. I like it here. Daddy always told me stories about Miss Camille's house, but I never believed. Not really."

"And now that you've seen it?"

"It's all true in the most wonderful way."

Her eyes lit up. It made me feel like a heel for questioning everything so much, and I felt even more out of place looking at her. Polly was thriving here, embracing the strangeness around us, and I was still trying to grasp at straws. Every time I reached something and squeezed it in my hands, it liquefied and ran out between my fingers.

A blackbird, a crow as it were, lighted on the railing of the porch. He was a large bird, bigger than a crow ought to be. He looked directly at me and then to Polly and back at me. If I didn't know better, I would have wagered he was sizing us up.

After he fixed his gaze on Polly, she shut her book and slid closer to him. The bench swing moved just a little as she inched along. She was moving very slowly as to not spook the thing, but I knew as well as anyone he would flap away when she got too close. Birds didn't trust people for a good reason.

After Polly had made it to the end of the swing, the crow hopped on the armrest closest to her. He let her reach out and pat his head. I'd never seen a bird so willing to be touched. Polly was very gentle, but still, most birds would never allow that in a thousand years.

"He's a lovely boy, isn't he?" asked Camille.

She appeared behind us in the doorway. We all jumped. Even the crow leapt up and landed back on the railing.

"Yes," Polly said. "Such a nice fellow."

"I see he's taken a liking to you. How about you come out and meet them proper, Crow. They ain't used to this. Probably think you're just a bird."

The crow tilted his head this way and that as if considering her words. I couldn't help but wonder what Camille was talking about. She had said something about another person who lived here. Someone by the name of Crow? She couldn't possibly mean...

"Come on now. Don't be shy," coaxed Camille.

The bird squawked in response. Then, he leapt into the air and flew away from us and the porch. We watched him speechless as he soared toward the barn. He was such a graceful bird. None of us began talking again until he flapped up to the hayloft window and disappeared from view.

"He ain't a crow?" I asked Camille.

"Well, he is most of the time. Wasn't how he was born. He's a Navajo boy named Crow. This is just how he prefers to be when new people are around."

"He turns into a crow?" asked Polly.

"Yes, in a manner of speakin'. Don't pay him no mind. Crow will relax and get used to you bein' here. He's just transitioning. It's good he came to visit you at all. I figured we wouldn't see much of him for months. Means he's interested."

"I don't understand..." I began.

"And you won't for a while. I told you boy. Stop trying to figure everything out at once. It will all come to you when it decides to. For now, I could use your help. Both of you."

"What do you want us to do?" asked Polly.

"Well, I just got the east side of the house snowing. It's finally starting to stick with the ground being as warm as it is. I could use your help planting my roses."

CHAPTER TEN

It truly was snowing on the east side of the house. Really. We turned the corner, and the temperature dropped sixty degrees. In a small, isolated spot a tiny cloud hovered above no higher than the roof. It couldn't be more than twelve feet any which way you measured it. The cloud kept a constant flurry of snow falling gently down just below it.

Snow was indeed sticking and building upon the grass against the house in minuscule drifts. To move a few feet in any direction would put you right back in the hot Texas sun, yet right here, we shivered with snow up to our ankles. There were two coats with gloves hanging from hooks on the wall. Camille grabbed them and handed one to me and one to Polly. Grateful, we both put them on before our fingers turned blue. The coats and gloves were far too big, but it was better than having nothing. I huffed a long breath that showed up as white fog in the frosty air. Everything smelled cold somehow, and it stung the inside of my nose.

Camille buttoned a rather large coat around herself in the brightest red fabric I've ever seen that seemed to glitter when she moved. She looked like a giant stick of cinnamon candy. After digging her hands in her pocket, Camille produced several packets of seeds wrapped in cheesecloth. We stuck out our hands instinctively as she handed one packet to each of us.

"What are these?" I asked.

"Seeds, of course. Rose seeds," replied Camille.

Ever so gently, she opened the delicate cheesecloth pouch in her hand. There were about a dozen perfect, little seeds in her palm. We looked at them with a sense of awe without knowing why exactly. When one observes a thing of beauty so tenderly produced, one had no choice but to admire. They were beautiful seeds; dark blue ones with the tiniest speckles of white. Like looking into a night's sky full of stars.

"What are these called?" asked Polly. "I've never seen seeds like them."

"These are a special type of rose. When it blooms, it really is something to behold. Light pink on one side of the petals and yellow on the other. Their real name is *A Better Tomorrow*. Isn't that a nice name to call a rose?"

Before we could answer, Camille knelt down in the building snow drift and dug a small hole in the snow. Ever so carefully, she placed one of the seeds inside it before covering it over with snow. Polly and I watched her do this a few more times, occasionally checking in with one another to make sure we were both watching the same thing.

"Miss Camille, why are you putting the seeds in the snow?" asked Polly.

"Because these seeds are from Australia. Clear on the other side of the world," she replied.

"What's that got to do with planting seeds in the snow?" I asked.

"Clear on the other side of the world is winter time right now. Can't expect an Australian rose to bloom out of its own season. I'm just making them feel right at home."

I was pretty darn certain that wasn't how seeds worked, but so much else in this place seemed off, there was no point arguing this one. For her part, Polly agreed to go along with the task. Fighting the bulk of our over-sized sleeves, we planted beautiful seed after beautiful seed in the building snow drifts. When we finished, Camille slapped the snow from her mittens and smiled at her progress.

"There now, they are gonna bloom up pretty. *Vivian's Rose*. They'll be perfect."

"I thought it was called something else," I said.

"*A Better Tomorrow*," added Polly helpfully.

"Yes well, that be what other people call it, but I call it *Vivian's Rose*. She might not ever see them, but they are for her."

CHAPTER ELEVEN

The whole house woke up to Polly's screams. I bolted upright in my bed when I heard it. Nothing like the sound of a girl's scream to make your heart revive racing. It was nearly dawn; I could tell by the orange light and the crisp smell of dew wafting from the window. Another wailing broke the air. This wasn't just a shriek from a bad dream or the panic of a shadow startling her. A deep fear coursed through her voice, shrill and panicked.

I was the first into her room, feeling glad she hadn't locked it. My eyes scanned the room in an utter panic to find no one in it at all. The room appeared to be empty, yet the screaming continued. I spun in place, searching for its source. There was no Polly.

A thought occurred to me. What if Polly's father had come in the night and stolen her from her room? What if he was holding her just on the other side of the window?

I raced to the window, throwing back the curtains, and looked outside. Not only was no one there, but the window was shut and locked from the inside. The ghost of Polly kept crying. Finally, the notion of calling her name slapped me across the face.

"Poll! Poll, where are you?"

"Nat please help me!"

"Where are you? I can't see you."

"Under the bed…sort of."

I got down on my hands and knees next to her four post bed and craned my neck to look underneath. It took me a minute to find her. The expectation was to find her body jammed underneath, face pinched against the mattress above. That wasn't what I saw.

What I found first was her face. There was no other way to describe it other than it was poking down from under the mattress. Not like there was a hole or a tear in the mattress; her face looked to be a part of the bed. When I considered things closer, I saw some locks of her hair and fingers were also somehow sticking out of the bottom of the mattress. It wasn't unlike when someone floats belly up in murky water, and all you could see of them was the parts that stuck up. The rest of their body was obscured by water. In this case, the mattress hid Polly's body the way water did. One hand was even coming through one of the bed boards. It was all impossible.

She locked eyes with me, terror lighting them up like a firecracker. Her fingers twitched as she tried to pull herself free. I sat up and checked the top of the bed for the rest of her body, but it wasn't there either. Polly was wholly encompassed by her own bed.

"Poll, what happened? How'd you get like this?"

"I don't know. Oh God, I don't know!"

"Okay, okay. Calm down. Does it hurt?"

"No, but I can't move anything."

A shadow made its presence known on the opposite of the bed as me. It moved and shuffled as the owner got on their hands and feet. I had never been so relieved to see Camille's face staring back at me from the other underneath the other side of the bed. She looked from me to Polly and assessed the situation.

"Help, Camille. I don't know what happened. Please. I can't move," said Polly, trying to manage her panic.

"What's happening to her?" I asked, trying to keep a lid on my own fear.

Camille didn't say anything at first. She merely examined Polly and stood up to look at the top of the bed the way I had. When she returned to us, she wasn't smiling or panicking. Camille was more neutral than I'd ever seen her. Somehow that made me more afraid.

"Camille, what's happening? We got to get her out of there!"

"I know, I know. Be calm, child. Fidgeting and flailing is only gonna make this worse."

"Worse? How could this be worse?" squeaked Polly.

"Calm, girl. Tell me, what book have you been readin' lately? From the library, I mean. The special books."

Polly's eyes grew huge. A kind of knowing brought tears to them. Camille nodded to her gently. They had some understanding I didn't. I was ten paces behind and hated it.

"Teleportation," whispered Polly.

"Okay. That's what I thought. You did this, honey."

"But…but I didn't."

"You didn't mean to, but you did. I never was skilled at it, but from what I understand, Teleportation is all about relaxing enough to move your matter through something else. You probably relaxed in your sleep and moved through the mattress. You woke, it scared you, and now you're stuck."

"Oh, God. Oh, Damn it. My daddy said this place would kill me," said Polly, tears falling from her face and splashing in little puddles on the floor. "And I'm not 'spose to say damn," she added, crying harder.

"You ain't gonna die. This just means you're learning to use this new skill. That's good. You got yourself in this mess. You can get out of it," said Camille gently.

"How do we get her out?" I asked.

"We don't. We are only here to help her do it. Here Nat, put your hand here," said Camille pointing to place where Polly's left hand poked through. "I'll get her right one. Now, Polly, you gotta repeat what you did to get in here to get out. Okay?"

"But I don't remember doing this!" cried Polly. "I was sleepin'. I don't know what I did."

"You got the skill, honey. Or else the book wouldn't have appeared to you. Your heart knows what to do. It's your head that's in the way. I want you to relax and close your eyes."

Polly blinked away a few more tears and shut her eyes. Her tiny fingertips still trembled in my hand. I hated this. My body ached to pull her out or hack away at the bed with an axe until she was free.

"Okay, good. Take a deep breath in and out. There you go."

I watched as she took one big inhale and exhale after another. The pinched line in between her eyes relaxed a little. Her mouth started to soften.

"This is all about relaxing. Imagine you are on the surface of a calm sea. Your breath is holding you on the surface. The air in your lungs keep you steady. Are you feelin' it?"

"Yes," Polly said in a trance-like voice. "I'm floating."

"Floating feels good, doesn't it? Safe?"

"Yes."

"You control where you go."

"I control where I go," Polly repeated.

"That's exactly right. The breath in keeps you here, but a good breath out moves you in the water. It lets you sink in the water. You are in control of all of it. Say that now," coached Camille.

"Yes. I am in control."

"Okay then. That's good. I want you to take an easy breath in. That keeps you where you are. Now, I want you to slowly let it out. When you do, relax your body. Let yourself sink in the lake. Your body will move for you."

Polly kept her eyes shut as she took a deep breath in and held it. Then, she let out the air in a steady pace, relaxing her face and fingers. The strangest thing happened. As soon as she started the exhale, Polly began emerging from the bed. Her body moved fluidly down and away from the mattress. She sank into the lake of her mind, moving through the confines of her furniture. Camille and I gripped her hands and elbows as they emerged to keep her from smacking her nose on the floor.

I couldn't believe what I was watching. Polly couldn't believe it either. She didn't seem to realize what had happened until her feet plopped on the floorboards with a thud. Her eyes flew open as she turned her head to face me. Tears streamed down her face as she smiled bigger than I'd ever seen from her. She had done it. She had moved through the bed to freedom.

My arms grabbed her elbows and helped her drag her body out from underneath the bed. When she stood up to face me, her astonishment turned into a kind of joy. Those hazel eyes of her lit up with excitement, all traces of tears having been erased. The room turned electric.

"I did it!" she shouted to me.

"You did!" I shouted.

We both turned around to see Camille standing on the other side of the bed with a huge grin on her face. She was proud, so very proud.

"I did it, Miss Camille," said Polly. "I did it myself."

"You sure did, sugar."

Camille opened her arms out, her orange dressing robe flaring out like a pair of silk wings. With the sun peeping in through the window, she almost glowed. All apprehension of the peculiar house or her intentions melted in that moment. Nothing but loving, nothing but kindness, nothing but acceptance. Such a rare thing I hadn't seen in years of riding the trains. A weight lifted in my heels; a tension in my arms calmed. I wanted to race to her too, to let her embrace me with her warmth. My skin itched with it. I practically stood on my toes wanting it. But this wasn't my comfort. It was for Polly, not me. I wasn't invited.

Polly ran to her, throwing her tiny body an orange embrace. The silk wings enveloped her. They hugged and rocked back and forth together. I kept to the wall, trying not to intrude. When Polly finally pulled away, she was practically jumping from excitement.

"I can do it again. I know I can!"

"Wait Poll. Maybe you shouldn't," I said trying to stop her.

Camille waved me off silently. She walked over to the wall that held the door to the hallway. With a little pat on the wall, she motioned for Polly to join her.

"I bet you can, pumpkin. Try on the wall. It's a bit easier for practice."

Without hesitation, Polly walked over to the wall. She paused at it as though she were having second thoughts, but even from behind her, I could see the deep breaths she was taking. She was preparing to give it a go.

"That's it. Just like with the lake. Breathe in…..and out," said Camille.

Polly took an exaggerated breath in and then stepped forward on the exhale. She walked right through the wall and disappeared. I ran to the door and looked out into the hallway. I found Polly there jumping up and down for joy. I couldn't believe my eyes.

"Do it again. Do it back in here," I said, getting just as excited as the girls.

She nodded and faced the wall. With another big breath, Polly moved through the wall and back into her room. I met her inside, and we jumped up and down. Well, I jumped, and she tried. Her enthusiasm was temporarily hindered by the tail of her nightgown getting trapped in the wall. She turned around and tugged at it irritated.

"You can't get lazy with it, girl. You'll leave bits behind," said Camille laughing.

Polly nodded to her, shut her eyes, and pulled the fabric out on a long breath. She was free, and we were left to talk excitedly in the calm of the morning. We were like hens gabbing with one another. Well, it started out that way at least. The three of us chattering about what Polly did. But then, it was just two. Camille and Polly sat together on the bed and held hands, leaving me standing as the outsider just a foot away.

I didn't really believe they meant to. No one pushed me away or asked me to leave. It was just their way of talking. Excitement slipped so easily in details of magic and what it felt like. They were two extraordinary people discussing something I didn't know. What else could I have said to keep up, to fit in with them? Again I stood alone trying to blend with the wall. In the end, maybe that was my only power, blending into things as though I were cellophane.

"Can you believe it, Miss Camille? I did it. I mean I really did. It was me. I never did anything like that. I'm magical!"

"Of course you are, dear. You found your magic. It's a wonderful day. There is so much to learn now! You won't believe what doors this opens. I can't wait to show you."

I had nothing to say other than congratulations. So far, there was nothing special in me at all. Just a boxcar kid who looked after a girl and got lucky enough to find a room somewhere. I stood there and watched the two amazing women in front of me who could do impossible things. They were so happy. I should have been too, but once the excitement wore off, all I had left was jealousy.

An outsider yet again, I let myself out of Polly's room. They didn't even notice I'd gone.

Chapter Twelve

When I stormed into the library, it was blessedly empty of people. The only soul who tried to speak to me on the way there had been Buck in the cold study. Not even his remarks about my needing to ask permission to enter his domain slowed me down.

I threw open the library door in a huff. Maybe in a different moment, I would have found the scene pretty. Early dawn light poured in the huge windows, casting purple shadows beneath every pillow and chair. The books all had a golden tint to them from it, like they too were waking up. Angel dust motes danced but only in the rays of light. Tiny bits that looked like something living. Everywhere else, they were invisible.

The pretty scene wouldn't deter me. I had a head of steam fueled by the exclusion of the morning, and I wasn't ready to give it up. If Polly could walk through walls, there had to be something I could do. The idea I was the only one ordinary in the house crashed down on my thoughts like a hammer. I had to be special; I just had to be.

I went to the bookshelf and pulled the first volume my hand rested on. It was a smaller book, green in appearance and bound in the corners with tweed. When I opened it to the titles page, I waited almost a whole minute, hoping words would appear to me. Shutting my eyes, I counted the seconds as they ticked by. One, two, three, four. I practiced my breathing like Polly had done earlier. Keeping myself calm was the key. The words would appear with patience.

They didn't. The page stayed blank.

After shutting the book with a bang, I threw it to the floor. Again I looked for another book. This was a larger one, blue with gold trimming. I opened it to the title page and waited. Only this time, it was only a few seconds.

Nothing appeared. I threw it to the ground like the other one.

My next victim was a dark maroon book so thick I had to use both hands to pull it from the shelf. I was so frustrated, I didn't try the title page. I opened the book, fanning the pages in front of me, looking to catch the whisper of a word inside.

There was nothing. It was always blank. A million books with a million blank pages silently laughing at me. Everyone could read them but me. I was alone in a sea of spectacular, set adrift because nothing about me had a place there.

The anger welled up. Every bit of fear, frustration, confusion, and bitterness. It all started in my gut and radiated outward until my body felt hot. Renewed energy jolted my muscles. A feverish heat burned the backs of my eyes. Nothing had made sense here. Nothing at all. This made even less sense. I'd had enough.

I tore a book from the shelf. Without bothering to open it, I threw it to the ground. Another book and another. I grabbed two or three at a time and hurled them to the floor. Screaming with frustration, I dug my hands in between volumes and pushed whole rows to the ground.

Sweat gathered around my neck and rolled down my back. I panted and grunted as my lungs tried to keep up. The destruction felt so good. So much release. Fighting back felt better than anything. I inhaled fire and breathed out smoke. Even box car trash had a place. Even we get a chance at something better.

"Now, that ain't no way to treat a library."

I spun around, still breathing hard and spitting rage. To my surprise, Nan stood in the doorway. It was so familiar, the way she appeared and where she stood. She had been in that exact spot the first time Polly and I found the library. Something about it froze my rampage, the familiarity of it.

She leaned against the doorframe looking at me and the mess I'd made. It wasn't a reproachful face but one of disappointment. Just facing her stole the heat from my body. My limbs relaxed, and the heat vanished. Around me was a pile of books, mistreated and abused. For the life of me, I couldn't understand why I had done it. All that rage had come and gone and what had it left? Nothing but destruction and shame. I slumped into myself.

"I...I'm sorry, Nan. I just..."

"You just what, child?"

I looked down at my hands as if they had the words for me. They didn't of course. Hands were only good for doing and not thinking. I shook my head and plopped down on a nearby pillow. What had I done?

"I just...don't belong here," I said at last. "I think I should leave."

It didn't seem possible, how fast she made it across the room to me. When I bowed my head, she was in the doorway. By the time I looked back up, she was in the armchair next to me, a motherly hand on my shoulder. She was wearing light blue gloves today made of soft cotton. It felt like being touched by a dandelion before the seeds blew away.

"How did…?" I started to ask but then decided against it. The answer would probably just make me more miserable. Another fantastical thing performed by someone better than me.

"You didn't like it here when you first came 'round. I know you didn't. My room scared you so bad, you ain't been able to get near it since," said Nan. "The place can be a bit much on a system unaccustomed to the bizarre. Doesn't mean you don't belong or you should leave."

"Nothin' makes sense here to me," I confided. "Nothin' at all. Every time I think I got a handle on a solid bit, somethin' else shows up and knocks me over again."

"Can't get a sure footing?"

"Yes, that's exactly it. Can't make heads or tails out of anythin' here. I never feel steady."

"Then, tell me why you're breakin' my library?"

There was no malice in her voice. No hint of retribution or admonishment to come. That seemed almost worse somehow. I'd rather she yell at me.

"I don't know. Polly, she can walk through walls now. We found her stuck inside her bed this morning. *Inside* her bed. I didn't think a thing like that was possible."

"That's good. You should be happy for her," said Nan.

"I am…I was. But why? Why did she get a book the first day? We came here together, and she's already walkin' through walls. I can't even get a book to show me somethin'."

"So, your mad because you can't understand this place but also mad because you can't do somethin' special?"

"It sounds awful dumb when you say it like that," I said moping.

"It ain't dumb, child. You're worried you ain't special. A natural reaction if ever I heard one. You are gonna be fine."

"But…what if I can't do anything? What if I never fit in?"

"Child, let me tell you somethin'. Every person on this earth can do somethin' special. Every single one. Each baby is born with gift inside them to do amazing things. Call it magic, call it whatever you like, but everyone is capable of doing somethin' spectacular."

"If that's true, why ain't folks walking around doing things like you all the time?"

"Because life as we know it tells us we can't from the second we walk to the minute we die. Every day, whether you know it or not, folks are remindin' you how ordinary you are, how you don't matter more than another leaf on a tree. After a while, you get used to the idea."

"Everyone has magic. That don't make sense."

"Oh no? What about people who sense a storm is comin' without any warning? A parent who can tell their child is in danger when there's no way of knowing. The man with a mind so special he can see how to invent something that never existed before. A woman so amazing she can understand the science of a world too small to see with your eyes. These are not examples of magic? Of folks doing amazin' things?"

"But I ain't ever met people like you. Like Camille."

"You might have," said Nan contemplating the idea. "They hide in plain sight like we do. We try to make safe havens for people like you and Polly who need them. Show you the way things could be if you just let them be."

"So you are one of these people. Is Camille your daughter?" I asked and then realized how rude it must sound. "If you don't mind me asking."

"I don't mind, and no, she ain't. I truly wish I could claim her as mine. Camille is a thing all to herself. She came to me on the wind."

"And Jacob? Is he her son? I never see him leave that table."

Nan snickered a little.

"No, he's not her son. And you will never see him leave that table. He doesn't have to or want to. That's his place."

"I don't understand."

"Child, that's your problem. You gotta stop tryin' to understand. Your reckonin' don't always work here."

"But Polly...?" I tried to protest.

"Polly came from a place different than you or me. Her world was one where people told her what to do every day. They told her how to live, how to breathe, how to think. She was a possession there and not a person. When she came here, she was an open pitcher, just waiting to be filled. She ain't seen much of the world at all. Hadn't had to live in it, make sense of things on her own. Accepting what is in front of her as true ain't a new thing for her."

"And me?"

"You've seen some things, child. I can see it on you a mile away. You've had to live a life in the world and fend for yourself before your time. Makin' sense of the world kept you alive. You were good at it. Strong for it. Now you can't make sense of this, and it's hurting."

I lowered my head and nodded. She put her gloved hand out and tickled my scalp with her bony fingers. The cotton slid around under my hair in a gentle, soothing way. Nothing could compare to the touch of someone trying to care for you. Just having someone to understand, even when I didn't, made all the difference to me.

"Will I ever be able to see words in the books?" I asked

"Yes, you will. Most souls are born from eggs hatched in the mouth of God. When they are born, they can speak the words of God because they knew the language before they ever opened their eyes to this world. The words are there inside everyone because they were there from the beginning."

"What does that mean?"

"Your words are buried under the years like seeds, child. When you relax and stop trying to understand everything, they will come to you. They'll blossom like those sunflowers out yonder. That's when you'll know them, and the books will open for you. I have a feeling about you, you know. When they do appear, it will be beautiful," said Nan with a glowing smile.

I thought about that a moment. Everyone had the ability to be special. Could that be true? Might every person on Earth be capable of great things?

"What about bad people?" I asked.

"Bad people? What do you mean?"

"Bad people. Can they do magic? Could they see the words in a book? If we are all hatched in the mouth of God, what about bad people like Polly's father? What about his words?"

Nan pulled a sour face and leaned back in the plush armchair.

"Folks like that have walked the dark road too long. Their words have rotted away."

CHAPTER THIRTEEN

I kept to myself for the next few days. Partly because I was still sour about the library and partly because I needed the time to clear my head. Nan said I had to try to not understand for a while. It was a hard habit to let go.

Mainly, I kept to my room reading the novels that kept appearing on my shelves and swiping food from the kitchen whenever I felt hungry. I tried reading *Moby-Dick* by Herman Melville. It looked like a good adventure story, but I kept feeling sorry for the whale and couldn't finish it. As soon as I gave up on the book and set it down on my bed, it vanished in front of my eyes.

When I finally decided to venture out to find Polly, she was sitting on the white porch swing in the back of the house. A large crow was perched on the back of the swing as though it were visiting. Polly had her book out, and she was reading to the bird. He a shy student and she an attentive teacher.

She waved her fingers in the air, shoved them through the book and wiggled them on the other side. It reminded me of a traveling magician I'd seen in Missouri except Poll didn't need a curtain for the trick. The smile on her face was infectious, and the crow squawked and flapped his wings. Polly laughed as though they had just shared a good joke.

I made my presence known by slowly walking up to them. The crow eyed me suspiciously at first, but Polly waved me over, seeming happy I was there. She scooted over and patted the space on the bench next to her. I accepted the invitation and sat down gingerly as to not chase off the crow.

"I was just telling Crow all about this teleportation thing. Ain't it the best?"

"It is that," I said forcing a smile.

Polly caught the strain and forced me to meet her eyes.

"What's wrong? I ain't seen you the past few days. Are you sick?"

"Na. I'm just a heel," I said.

"No you're not. You're beautiful," she said softly.

It was so gentle and sincere. The words took my breath away. No one had ever called me beautiful before, at least, not that I could recall. Polly reached her small hands over me and grabbed my hand.

"Don't worry. Nan told me you don't think you're special. You are. I know it," she said patting my hand between hers.

The smile that spread its wings across my face was effortless. What a fool I had been to hide away from her so long. I looked into the eyes of my friend, and she smiled back. The crow cawed and made a scene over jumping off the swing and flapping away. The swift breeze he left in his wake smelled of grass and wildflowers.

"Oh now, Crow. I think you're beautiful too. Come back here!" called Polly.

He didn't look back, just soared across the garden and flew up to the barn window.

"I think he's mad. What do you think?" she asked.

"Hard to tell with a bird. Never could get a feel for them," I replied.

"I like birds. We didn't have many of them at the colony. All my brothers like to kill them with guns and slingshots cuz they got in the garden. Cook 'em up like little chickens," said Polly with a disgusted face.

"That place you're from, the colony, Camille said it's bad. Like a cult or something."

"I don't know what it is. I can't say really. It's all I knew before here."

"What was it like?" I asked scooting closer to her. "Don't tell me if you don't want to. I don't mean to pry."

"Of course I'll tell you. I just love talkin' now. Here, I can say anythin'. My old home they said I gabbed too much. Wasn't right for a girl, so I'd run off and do it anyways with my sisters. The colony was alright most of the time, I suppose. I only left because I came of age."

"Came of age?"

"Fifteen. I had my fifteenth birthday a month ago. That means I get married off to one of the men. Everyone said I was so lucky because Brother Matthew wanted me. He's a high elder, even higher than my daddy."

"But you didn't want to marry him I take it?"

"He's old, even older than daddy. Already got four wives, and none of them are really alive anymore. They're breathin' and walkin' around, but all the light's gone from their eyes. His fourth one used to watch me and brothers and sisters. She was so fun, told stories from some special book she found. We played games and sang songs. As soon as she came of age, he took her, and she was never alright after that."

"What happened?"

"The hurtin' that happens to girls when they get married. She didn't sing after that or play games. She just sort of went all hollow, like the part of her that made her happy flew away. I would've been wife number five. I just couldn't stay."

"Couldn't you just say no? Couldn't she just say no?"

"There is no sayin' no where I'm from. At least, not for the girls. I wasn't supposed to read as much as I did there either. We are taught enough to read the good book. My brother Luke was the one that slipped me other books. He's the one that helped me with the witch part."

"What do you mean the witch part?"

Polly took a deep breath in and let it out in a gust. There was some water rimming her eyes while she thought about her brother. Her lip trembled a little as she tried to compose herself enough to speak his name. I winced watching her miss him so much.

"Daddy was so mad I didn't want to marry. He said I was an awful demon of a girl, and I'd do it whether I liked it or not. Daddy didn't want to lose face in front of the other elders. But what he said gave me this idea. The idea to trick everyone into thinkin' I was a witch. If I was a witch, no one would want to marry me."

"You're the one who did that? You chained yourself to the post?"

"No, but I made them think I was a witch. Luke helped me. Found me a book about how our people spot a witch among the women. It was an old book we found in the men's library. Most clues were silly things, like arguing with my sisters too much and talking gibberish."

"Talking gibberish made them think you were a witch?" I asked with my eyebrows raised. "That sounds awful dumb."

"We thought so too. I already did that anyway. So, we pulled other tricks. Like I left a milk bottle out to sour, but I'd pretend it hadn't. When someone saw me drinking sour milk, I'd swear it was fine before I touched it. I told them it tasted fine to me, so they all thought my touch turned the milk bad."

"Oh yuck. You drank it sour?"

"There are worse things."

"Surely, that didn't do it? The sour milk thing?"

"No, it wasn't enough. As the weddin' day got closer, Luke said we had to do somethin' drastic. Everyone was gettin' things ready for the ceremony, so we had time to sneak around. I drew weird symbols all over my bed and the floor of my room with bits of charcoal. He got this mud that stains your skin all brown. He drew the same symbols all up and down my arms so it marked up my skin that way. It only lasted about a week, but that's all we needed. My daddy found me in bed spittin' and talkin' gibberish, stuff drawn all over me. The other elders came and declared me possessed. I was officially a witch."

"But you knew what they'd do. If you read the books, you had to have some idea they'd chain you to that post or worse. What if they burned you?"

"They wouldn't do that. Elder Matthew still wanted his fifth wife. The post was supposed to heal me. Starve the demon from me so I could atone for my evil ways. Luke brought me seeds and water when he could."

"You were hoping someone would find you," I said.

"I prayed someone would find me, or I could find a way to escape. Anythin' would be better than goin' back there. Then you came, and then Camille. I'm safe now. It worked. The two of you answered my prayers."

I thought about it in silence with her. She had to be so brave to pull a stunt like that. Abandoning all you ever knew to jump into an uncertain life. Perhaps it was some sort of fate that brought us together, some kind of magic. I knew exactly what it took to run away and how frightening it was. I'd done the same thing myself.

"What if they come for you here? Polly, I saw your daddy in town. He threatened Camille to give you back. He said he'd come claim you, and you'd have to atone. He was so angry. I think he'd burn the whole place down to get at you."

To my surprise, Polly smiled.

"That's why I got y'all to protect me," she said. I watched as her face turned darker, as though another thought nudged its way to the fore. "Besides, I'd rather burn than go back."

"Trust me, you don't want to burn," said a voice behind us.

The sudden sound of another voice startled us so much we jumped. Polly and I spun around in the swing. There, just on the other side of the porch, was an Indian boy just an inch shorter than me standing in the tall grass. He was completely naked with his hands crossed over his chest and a face that expected to be recognized.

CHAPTER FOURTEEN

The second shock came from Camille tapping her foot behind us on the floorboards of the porch. The empty knocking sound had Polly and me spinning like tops trying to look from one person to the next. My mind sparked electric. Nothing worse than being snuck up on. Even worse when it was from both sides. We were flanked.

"Crow, I told you there were clothes in the barn. These ones aren't used to so much dongle out in the breeze," said Camille in admonishing way. She set her hands on her hips in that way she did when she wasn't in the mood for an argument.

Crow merely nodded and walked back the way he came. His bare rump out for anyone to see. Polly averted her eyes and giggled into her hands. I joined in with her. There was no way to help it really. A naked boy walking openly as he pleased was a sight worth laughing about.

"Pardon him, you two. He spends so much time as a bird, he forgets polite human things. Ah, there he is. Now we can all meet proper like."

The boy walked back up to us in a determined fashion. A pair of buckskin trousers covered him to the waist, and a loose linen shirt was thrown over his chest. He scratched at the seams, as though the notion of wearing clothes was wholly foreign to him.

"There now. That's better," said Camille with a smile. She moved closer to us. "Crow, I'd like you to formally meet Nat and Polly. Nat and Polly, this is Crow."

He nodded to us without a word. Polly and I smiled and nodded back. Tension set all of us on edge as we struggled for what next to say. I had seen a few Indians in my day along the tracks but never got to talk to any of them. They blended with the other men riding box cars like me. I'd jump a car and find groups of bedraggled men, all colors and types, passed out in moldy hay and reeking of whiskey. Most folks who ended up riding the rails drowned their sorrows in whatever they could find no matter what they looked like or where they came from. Personally, I tried to keep clear of the stuff because of my daily reminder of what could happen to a person.

The thought of the men I forced out of the train before Amarillo wiggled itself to the front of my mind. I could see their worn, terrified faces as I pointed my gun at them. All they wanted was my boots, and I might have had them killed for it. I shook my head to scramble the memory away and turned my attention back to the Indian boy in front of me.

The stories never ceased, the ones about the Indians. Sitting Bull and Crazy Horse. Old west stories about Geronimo and different tribes holding out as long as they could before their land was taken from them. They were heroic tales and sad ones. As far as I understood, most tribes lived on reservations now.

It occurred to me to ask about his tribe. They were all different. At least, I thought they were, but I didn't want to sound rude. What did I know about the ways of his people? I broke the silence with what I hoped was a polite question.

"What tribe are you? I mean your people? I don't know them well, I'm sorry."

Crow looked at me squarely. It was hard to tell what he thought from that face. He was sturdy and stoic, barely blinking when he looked my way. I could read no expression at all. For a brief moment, I thought it looked like a bird's face, emotionless. Maybe some of the bird had seeped into him. Maybe too much of it had.

"Navajo," he said without elaboration.

The good thing was he didn't sound mad.

"Crow here is a Navajo from far away. A skinwalker to be exact," said Camille, trying to fill the awkward silence with something of substance.

Polly's eyes lit up again, all hazel and gold. She turned an excited face to Crow and leaned toward him. I felt her small body tip the swing as she looked past me to him. It creaked beneath us as the weight shifted.

"That's why you can do that? Turn into a crow?" she asked.

"Yes, it allows me to change whenever I like," he said.

"Wow," whispered Polly in genuine awe.

Polly's enthusiasm was so childlike, so innocent. Even Crow fell victim to it. The stoic Navajo boy's face relaxed. His eyes grew wider when he looked at her. I even thought I caught the beginnings of a smile. Crow blinked a few times.

"Yes, our Crow here is really something special," said Camille. "Can you believe I found him picking strawberries? Of all things."

"Really? How'd you find him? Please tell me," said Polly.

She gaped from Camille to Crow and then back again. Polly was a kid at story time, and I was getting close up seats to her entertainment.

"Well, I was collecting some strawberries about a year or so ago, and I heard this song like a bird but not exactly. When I turned around, there was Crow pecking away at an overripe strawberry that had fallen to the ground."

"How'd you know he was a...what did you call it?" asked Polly.

"A skinwalker," provided Crow.

"Yes that."

"Well, I didn't at first. Then I saw this little flicker in his eyes when I got up close. Real birds can't do that. And his song, it had more to it than a regular crow's. Something deeper. The problem was he was flapping around, tripping all over himself." said Camille, her arms flapping about. "He'd hurt his wing."

Crow watched her and set his face with a hard line for a mouth. It was hard to tell, but this must have been what it looked like when he was embarrassed. I suppressed a laugh to lessen his humiliation. When Camille had stopped her own laughing, she continued the story.

"Anyway, I could tell he needed help, so I said, 'Boy, you best come over here and let me see you. I can mend an arm, but I ain't fit for feathers.' It worked. He turned back into a boy, dongle and all. I brought him back here and fixed him right up. Been with me ever since."

"How far did you have to travel?" I asked. "I mean, to get here."

"Far. Very far," he replied simply.

"As a crow or a boy?" asked Polly.

"As a crow. Easier to travel that way. I can fly and don't need as much food."

I couldn't help but imagine how much easier travel would be if you could fly. Soaring for hours on the wind. Anywhere and everywhere could be your destination. No trains, no boxcars, no men threatening you in the night. I blinked very hard as the faces of those two men appeared again, stuffing them back down into the dark places in my mind.

"How did you get to be a skinwalker?" Polly asked suddenly with stars in her eyes.

The mood changed in an instant. Crow's face, which had been gentle while looking at her, turned hard in a second. He glared at the two of us. It was so unexpected, I heard Polly gasp next to me. All my muscles tensed for whatever was to come next. The look on his face told stories of violence.

Camille stepped forward with her hand out to calm him.

"Crow, calm down. She doesn't know. She didn't mean anythin'."

His whole body was angry and tense. I prepared myself to face off against the boy as soon as he made a move at her. To my utter surprise, Crow arched his back, rolling into a ball in the air. A blackbird took his place. In a blink, he went from flesh and bone human to crow with only a scattering of feathers to show for it.

"Come on now. No need to fly off in a huff. They are white children. They don't know these things," pleaded Camille as the blackbird flew away from us.

It was of no use. Crow flew away and back to the barn. We watched him until the flicking of his tail feathers vanished into the barn window. All that was left of his human presence was a pile of barely worn clothes and the smashed grass where he had stood only minutes ago.

CHAPTER FIFTEEN

"I swear to about three things holier than me, I don't know why I bother keeping clothes around for that boy. He'd rather be a bird than eat a cake," said Camille as she stooped to gather the clothes he left in the grass.

The swing started shaking beneath me. It was slight, just a shimmer of movement. When I looked over to Polly to see if she felt it too, I saw that she was the one causing the rumble. Poor thing was trembling next to me, wide eyes filled with tears.

"I...I...I didn't mean to hurt him, Miss Camille. I don't know what I said, but I'm awful sorry," said Polly.

"Don't you worry about him. Crow will come back. He'll fly around, nearly get his head torn off in the process, and come back just as sociable as ever," Camille said sarcastically.

"You said he's a skinwalker," I said trying to make some sense of the whole thing. "What does that mean? Why'd he get so mad when Polly asked him?"

Camille let out a long breath and regarded us like she was suddenly very tired. She pulled a nearby wicker stool over to us and sat down. That big smile of hers was hidden beneath drooping eyelids and fading laugh lines.

The sun was getting lower in the sky, signaling the evening would come soon. With that came dancing colors and insects. Biting bugs that snuck up on a body and left only a welt behind. Yet, no mosquitos began their buzzing around us. In fact, had I thought about it, I hadn't been bitten once since I set foot in Camille's world. What else might a person call this place? It wasn't truly just house here. This was a world unto itself.

It wasn't until Camille patted Polly's knee that I noticed she was crying. Polly's shaking had ceased, but heavy tears rolled down her face one right after another. The poor girl was trying not to show it or make a sound. I handed her a handkerchief from my pocket.

"Enough of that now. If you want me to tell you the story, you gotta stop that cryin'. I can't stand for my stories to be outdone by a weeping lady. Come on now."

Camille smiled at Polly, and Polly sniffed back some tears that were on their way out and nodded her head. I patted her hand.

"Alright then. Now, I'll tell you, but it's best not to talk to Crow about it."

"Why?" I asked.

"You'll see after I'm done," she said with a pause. Camille shut her eyes for a moment and inhaled deeply. Something in her settled, and she nodded to acknowledge it. "This is a hard thing to talk about. Folks like you ain't even supposed to hear these words. If I give them to you, you keep them close. You hear me? No gabbin' this around."

We nodded. I don't think either of us really knew what she meant by that specifically, but the feeling was there, and we knew enough to agree. Besides, who would we tell anyway?

"Alrighty then. Crow is Navajo like he said. Navajo, Apache, Comanche, Sioux, Cherokee, all them lived in this land of America before us. They were hunted and round up by the white soldiers. They moved away again and again, but the soldiers closed in on them, making the Indian world smaller and smaller. Eventually, they were forced to live on reservations. So small were these places. Even smaller to people who were used to wide, open country. Some stayed, some didn't. Most hated the confinin' life on the reservations but were afraid to leave. Some were not afraid, like Crow and his family."

"They left the reservation?" I asked. "Wouldn't they get punished for that?"

"I don't know the whole story. I only was able to piece together the bits Crow would tell me and what Jacob saw on his chessboard."

I opened my mouth to ask about that, Jacob and his board. I still didn't understand the boy who never left the table and moved chess pieces around in a game he only played with himself. When I tried to interrupt with the question, Polly took my hand and stopped me. She squeezed it as if knowing what I wanted to say and discouraged me. Best talk about one mystery at a time.

"Based on the pieces, this is what I know. Crow set out from the reservation with his father and brothers. His mother had died from some disease they blamed on the white soldiers. A thing about cursed blankets. When they left, they took weapons with them."

Polly let go my hand to bring her hands up to her mouth. I grabbed one and held it again, squeezing until her heart calmed.

"I can't tell you what happened after that. Crow says they did nothing wrong. He says they were looking for their own way in the world. They were lost after his mother passed and wanted none of the life on the reservation. He also said the soldiers accused them of attacking towns and raiding armory sheds."

"Is that part true?" I asked.

"I don't know to be honest. He is guarded about it, and I don't push. I like having him here, and I want him to stay. He's safer here in the barn than he ever would be out there."

"Did? Did the soldiers go after them?" asked Polly tentatively.

A bit of darkness fell over Camille's face then. She nodded so slightly, we barely saw her do it at all. A tremble of foreboding zigzagged inside me. I had an inkling of what came next but didn't want it to be true, like when you read a book and know the hero is about to die.

"They came for them in the shadow of the night, the way most villains are want to do. Cowards do the same thing. Crow said they lit their camp on fire. Everything burned into flames, even one of the horses. The rest of the ponies charged away from Crow and his tribe, leaving no way for the men to get out."

"What did they do?" Polly asked.

"They fought. It was the only honorably thing to do. There would be no surrender. Besides, the soldiers didn't want surrender anyway. They were shootin' Crow's brothers and cousins all around him. Poor Crow was the youngest, and he ran to his father's tent for help. He found him there, already shot and bleedin' out. Crow had no choice but to help his father try to escape. He dragged him out and down a hill, away from the violence. Said he could see the camp on fire from far away so bright it looked like the sun was rising."

Camille reached out and placed her worn, callused hand on top of our hands. Three stones stacked on top of one another, ready to face the next part, the hero part.

"His daddy was bad off, but Crow didn't want to face it. He kept tryin' to drag him away. Eventually, the task was too hard, and his father couldn't go on anymore. He told Crow that there was nothin' to do for him now. It was his time to pass into the next world of their ancestors, where his mother was now. But the soldiers were comin'. They were tracking the blood his father left behind. It wouldn't be much time before they were upon them. So he told Crow to shoot him."

"To shoot him? Why? So the soldiers couldn't?" I asked in disbelief.

"No. I told you he was a skinwalker, but I didn't tell you what a skinwalker was. A skinwalker is a Navajo who kills one of their close family members. It is a grave sin in their world. To kill a family member means you will forever be cursed and take on the form of an animal."

"Crow killed his daddy?" asked Polly looking more and more petrified as the story went on.

"He didn't want to; he told me that. It haunts him. His father kept saying it was the only way to save himself. The only way to get away from the soldiers. They would catch a young Indian boy, but not an animal. They wouldn't look for an animal, especially not a crow."

"The soldiers, they were going to kill Crow," I added. "They were going to kill everyone."

"Yes. No reason to let the little one live. Just another witness. Another Indian kid to grow up hating them until he got old enough to be dangerous. And the soldiers were close, so close Crow could hear their footsteps. They didn't have much time, and his daddy pleaded with him. He was already dead, he said. There was no saving him, but he could save his last son. So Crow did it. He took his father's gun and finished the job the white soldiers started."

She didn't continue for a moment, allowing that part to sink in. I knew my mouth was hanging open, but all I could think about was Polly. Her little body had started trembling again. I squeezed her hand.

"Did the soldiers get him?" I asked.

"Almost. He waited until the last minute to do the deed, hoping something else might save them. The soldiers were almost on him when his father's spirit left the world. When it did, Crow's body turned into a bird right in front of the soldiers' eyes and flew away. They couldn't make heads or tails of what they saw. As far as anyone knows, they told their commander all the Navajo in the camp were killed."

"Miss Camille. I didn't mean…" started Polly so softly I could barely hear her. "I was…I didn't know about that part…"

It was getting later, and purple sunlight lit her from behind, casting little sparkles in the wet pools in her eyes. A few big tears ran down her face and splashed on my hand. Her face was wet and smelled of salt. My hand was still over hers, still trying to comfort, and not doing a very good job.

"Shush with that now," said Camille. "If I cried every time that boy flew from me in a huff, I'd be dry as the desert. You didn't know."

"He killed his own daddy," I said disbelieving, looking out at the silent barn.

"He did. It was the only way he could live, and he blames himself every day for it. That's his curse. He lived like his father wanted, but he's cursed with the guilt."

Something in the back of my brain niggled at me. It was like when you get a kernel of something stuck in your teeth and can't get it out no matter how much you tongue it. A whisper in my mind said the timing of this wasn't right.

"When did this happen, Camille? I mean, I ain't heard of any Indian revolts. I've been ridin' the rails a bit now, and no one talks about them like they used to. Not since pioneer days. Not since the wars. At least I thought so."

To my surprise, Camille winked at me and touched her nose.

"Quick thinking. You nailed that bit without me having to tell you," she said.

"Wait? It didn't happen recently? The soldiers I mean?" asked Polly.

"Honestly, I have no idea when this happened," said Camille. "I wish I did. Crow talks about it like it was a year ago it's so fresh in his mind, but his account is sketchy in the way of details. Certain things 'round here seem downright alien to him that he ought to know, and even though he's been with me for over five years, he hasn't changed much at all."

"Changed? You mean aged," I said, starting to catch on. "He doesn't look much older than me now, and he looked 'bout the same then."

Camille tapped her nose at me again.

"I don't think I understand," said Polly, looking back and forth between the two of us.

"Think about how you looked five years ago, Polly. I 'spect you were a might bit different looking. Not as tall and all that. You children change so much from year to year."

Polly looked down at her hands as if they were a way to measure her passing in the last five years. I decided to look at my own. Five years ago these hands were clean and smooth and cared for. Now they were worn and tough. Five years of hardness pounded into them. Grit permanently stained the skin under the nails. She and I both nodded for Camille to go on. We had indeed changed quite a bit in five years.

"Crow hasn't. Not much at all really. Which brought me to next part of the skinwalker legend I had only heard whispers of. Some say when a skinwalker is in their animal form, they don't age. They are as they are, frozen in time. Crow prefers to spend a lot of his time as a crow. I think it's easier on him somehow. If he's a boy, he'll have to converse in the world as people do, and that hurts under all the guilt he carries around him."

"But that means, he isn't aging when he's a crow. He only ages when he's a boy," added Polly.

"That's right. So the truth is I don't really know when this thing happened any more than I know how old Crow really is. I may never know. One day, I fear he will stop being a boy altogether and fly away from here, leaving his human skin behind."

CHAPTER SIXTEEN

Everyone was asleep the next morning when the storm rolled our way. I was the only one awake when it first made itself known to the world. At least, that's what I thought.

It came rolling in electric, charging the very air with static. I sat up in bed as the first glimpses of dawn light turned everything turquoise in my room. This feeling I knew. It was a hard thing to not know traveling as much as I had through the breadbasket of America. The rolling hammer of a dust storm was all too familiar to me, and one was heading our way. If we were really lucky, it might only bury parts of the house in dirt. If we're unlucky, it could bury us all alive.

All the tiny hairs on my arm stood on end. The gentle howling outside whispered frightening things on the horizon. When I touched the metal lamp on my bedside table, a shock of electricity arced to my fingertip.

I didn't bother with the window. No need to see what was coming to know its name. The dust storm would be upon us shortly, and I had to warn the others. I threw my clothes on in a whirl of fabric, not bothering too much with more than my undershirt. Not the smartest thing to do, but there wasn't any time. Besides, I doubt anyone would notice.

When I threw open the door, Camille stood in the hallway. She stared at me with wide eyes. I nearly jumped out of my skin at the sight of her.

"Camille! You scared me. You…"

"You felt it?" she asked.

There was no joy, no inflection to her. This was Camille frightened. It made everything about ten times scarier.

"Yes. Dust storm."

"Alright. Nothin' I can do about it. We gotta get the house shut up. I'll get Nan and Polly. Start boarding up the windows best you can. Start with Jacob's window. He won't move, so that's the first one to close."

I didn't need to say a word. Camille ran into Polly's room, and I went to the kitchen to find Jacob. He was in his usual seat spinning in place. I had never seen him nervous, but he was staring at me with fear in his face.

"Jacob, where is the wood Camille uses to shut these? I gotta get yours done before it hits us."

Jacob shook his head at me and pointed to the door. Never had he said a word to any of us, and I guess he wouldn't now either.

"I know I gotta go outside. Where is the wood? Are there panels?"

He shook his head again and pointed to the door. There was a rise in my belly, the foreboding kind. I didn't have time for this nonsense.

"Jacob, you gotta tell me! Talk!"

He shook his head harder and slammed his hand against the window frame. The understanding rammed into my brain like a sledgehammer.

"There are shutters? On the outside of the house?"

Jacob nodded, seeming both relieved and exasperated with me at the same time. I didn't waste time mincing words with a mute. I was out the door and into the waking world in an instant.

The dust storm was a wall of brown velvet in the distance. It hurtled closer and closer but looked impossibly still at the same time. I couldn't feel anything but the energy in my bones and the wind against my skin. Everything told me to run and hide. It smelled of dirt and blood and manure. This was a piece of God, coming to inflict its wrath on us all. The dawn was trying to lighten the horizon, fighting the good fight against this curtain of darkness.

There wasn't much time. I had to the take care of the house. To my surprise, there were no shutters on the windows. I was so frustrated, I slammed my firsts into the window frame. When I did, I was nearly thrown off my feet. A set of heavy shutters jutted out of the wall of the house and closed over the window. Once I regained my footing, all I had to do was latch and lock it down. It wasn't clear if it was another bit of magic or a marvel of technology I hadn't seen yet. Either way, I counted it a blessing.

I ran around the house playing this same routine. It wasn't until I latched every window I could find and the back door, that I went back in the kitchen. Jacob was hitting his hand on the table, trying to get my attention. He reached out to grab my sleeve and pulled me near. Jacob reached for a black knight and moved it forcibly to the middle of the board. His face told me I should know what he meant by this gesture, but for the life of me, I didn't.

"I don't know. What does this mean? I don't understand."

Jacob grabbed my hand and showed the knight to me again. It's little horse head sculpted in stone. Then, he knocked the piece over. I didn't know much about chess, but I did know that motion. It meant capture or death. Something bad at the very least.

"Someone's hurt? Someone's in trouble?"

Jacob tapped his nose the way Camille did, nodding his head with enthusiasm.

"Who, Jacob? Who's in trouble? I don't know who the black knight is. Tell me now. The storm is gettin' closer."

He looked around his table as though searching for a way to tell me. Finally, he joined his two hands together at the thumbs and spread the other fingers out. It wasn't until he made his hands flap like a bird that I realized who he was talking about.

Crow. He was out in the barn.

There was no time to talk. No time to explain. I threw myself out of the front door and into the wind. The world had become so violent so quickly. Dirt and grit pelted me from every angle, stinging my skin. I could barely breathe from it. What little progress the morning sun had made lightening the day had been snuffed out. I stumbled through a violent torrent in near blackness.

By the time I made it to the barn, I could already hear him coughing. I tried to slide the door shut behind me, but it was too hard against the wind. Crow climbed down from the hayloft on a ladder, nearly falling into me. He spat mucus and grit to the floor.

"I've got to get you to the house!" I shouted at him over the increasingly roaring wind.

"We have to help him," said Crow.

He pointed at Johnny Sander, the mule. There wasn't much to do for him. Poor Johnny stood in his pin, stomping around with unease. We couldn't take him in the house. It just wasn't possible. In the end, we blockaded the stall door with a few hay bales and tied down the tools. I threw a blanket over his back to help shield his hide. Crow patted his face and whispered words in his ears I could not make out. All that was left was to get out and latch the door.

The storm greeted us the second we left the shelter of the barn with a din of screaming and howling like I'd never heard. Crow and I were thrown to our backs. We scrambled back up only to get blown against the barn itself. It took a lot of effort and interlocking our forearms, but we managed to hang on long enough to slide the barn door shut and latch it.

Walking back to the house was less of a walk and more of a crawl. The lower we were, the less we resisted the wind. We could barely see a foot in front of our faces. I had to hold onto Crow's barefoot so as to not lose him.

I choked on the dust. He spit mud on the ground. There was no way to not breathe it in and hold it in your lungs. Nothing could keep it out. The dust built up in your lungs, layer by layer until it weighed you down. Pretty soon, we stopped trying to move forward. I had no idea where we were or how close we were to the house. Everything looked dark and hopeless.

We had about given up when I saw the light. It was a small thing at first and so very peculiar. Had I not known better, I would have thought it was a candle. An impossible thing, and I told myself as much. Then, it got closer and with it came a voice.

"Nat! Crow! Are you there?" yelled Camille into the roar of the storm.

It was impossible. There, just a few yards away, was Camille rushing toward us, holding a candle. I almost laughed. Out of all the unreal things I'd witnessed over the past weeks at her house, the sight of that tiny candle standing firm against the raging storm was by far the strangest.

Crow wasn't moving, and I barely could. The winds were choking us, and we weren't even close to the end of it. Death was coming. I could almost feel him sit his heavy bulk on my back, forcing me still so I might give up.

That's when everything stopped. The wind, the dirt, the suffocating weight. It all stopped. I wiped the grit from my eyes and looked up. Camille stood above us, that orange dressing-robe of hers barely moving in the wind. One hand held that impossible, little candle. It still shone brightly without even a flicker. Her other hand reached to the sky commanding something unseen. The scope of our sanctuary grew, and we managed to pull Crow in toward us and out of the rampage. I checked him in the dim light. He was barely awake and coughing up mud to the side. We rolled him on his side, and Camille slapped his back hard over and over again. Poor Crow vomited everything inside him. It was awful to see him wretch, but at least he was breathing in between gasps.

"Stop hitting me, Camille!" he sputtered as he rolled onto his knees.

I helped him to his feet, and we marveled at Miss Camille and her candle.

"How? How is…" I started to ask.

Camille raised the flame up so we could see above us. The storm raged on above and around us, but we were untouched. A vast river of dirt and rubble surging past on all sides. It sounded like a freight train tearing across the tracks. All around our party was a kind of bubble shielding us from the storm. We were surrounded and sheltered by a safety Camille had created.

Nan had said Camille came to her on the wind. I was beginning to understand why.

CHAPTER SEVENTEEN

We had managed to save Johnny Sanders from the dust storm, but a lot of the sundries had been misplaced or ripped apart. A trip to town was in order the following day, but Jacob wasn't having it. Every time Camille made to leave, he'd grab the black queen piece and slam it on the board, trying to get her attention.

"I know I know what the board says," said Camille patting his shoulder. "But I gotta go. No choice here. The storm swallowed up the extras, not to mention the garden."

Jacob slapped the table and shook his head at her.

"If I don't go now, Norman will sell all my things out from under me. It'll be weeks before he gets another shipment at this rate."

The boy wouldn't let up, glowering up at her. Camille crossed her arms over her chest and stared down at the little boy. He didn't flinch one bit under her scrutiny.

"It doesn't say checkmate, does it? Not even check. Just the danger of it."

Her imploring words fell on deaf ears. Jacob's glare didn't falter.

"What if I take Nat? How does that change everything then?" she asked with a little more honey in her voice.

She patted his shoulder gently, and Jacob regarded his board. Ever so slowly, he reached for the white knight and slid it to the side of the queen. The boy studied it for a minute before he relaxed the scowl on his face. When he gazed back up at Camille, his eyes were resolute.

"So, it'll be fine with him?" she asked.

Jacob nodded even though he didn't look pleased.

"Alrighty then. Nat, you're with me. Come on."

We hitched the wagon to Johnny Sanders, who had survived the great storm with only a few scratches from the wind beating in on him. The house had been hit, but most of it had been spared. Only a few damages to speak of other than the loss of the food. Not much in the way of dirt drifts piled up against the house. The windmill still stood, much to my surprise. I couldn't help but wonder if Camille had done her magic over the other parts of the house too.

As we started our journey to town, I began to see just how bad the storm was. Our little plot of land was clean compared to the rest of the world. Dust drifts four and five feet high collected against fence posts and sheds. Most of the grass was buried in it, leaving the prairie looking for all the world like the Mojave Desert. Even the flowers around the sign for *Miss Camille's House for Wayward Children* were barely visible above a pile of dirt. The sunflowers still bloomed as we passed by them. We could see the tops of their petals peeking out of the dust.

"Keep your wits about you when we get to town, Galahad. Jacob says there might be trouble," said Camille.

The rest of the ride was passed in silence. It seemed wrong to talk of pleasant things when so much had been destroyed the day before. Questions buzzed around my head like angry bees, but judging by the look on Camille's face, now wasn't a time to ask any. As we trotted along, every bit of damage we passed made her look older and tired. There was no sunshine in her cheeks, no stars in her eyes.

The town was buzzing when we got to the square proper. The storm had hit it, but not as hard as the farmland. Drifts of brown silt piled up against the buildings, but there had been more here to break the wind. More building with stronger foundations to provide sanctuary. Those families in the farmland were less protected.

The folks were skittish. It wasn't like before when they were afraid of the terrible Elder Jones terrorizing the town. These people were angry and afraid. The worst kind of combination. Men didn't move out of our way as they had before. Women didn't shuffle their children inside at the sight of the witch, Camille. What we got were glares and anger.

I felt the hate as did Camille. Her face, normally round from smiling, was long and serious. There was a slump in her shoulders I had never seen before, and she sort of turned in on herself as if to make herself smaller under their glares. Even Johnny Sanders snorted and jumped when a man spat on the road in front of us.

Before we got into the main square, we heard a friendly voice calling to us from a nearby alley. When we looked over, I saw the voice belonged to Norman, the general store manager. He was standing next to a small, squat woman. They both looked nervous, shoulders slumped as much as Camille's. Norman jumped from foot to foot.

"Miss Camille! This way!"

They motioned for us to park in the alley. Their stocky arms waving this way and that in a funny sort of manner. It reminded me of those puppet shows in the travelling circus. Motions too big to be real. Mr. Norman sure would make an awful conspirator.

The alley they squirmed in was plenty big enough, and Camille obliged them. No reason staying on the streets if we were so unwelcomed. Camille halted Johnny and jumped down as Norman took the reins. His hands were dirty like he hadn't washed them in weeks.

"What's goin' on, Norman? Why are we in an alley?" asked Camille.

"I was hopin' to catch you," said Norman in the loudest whisper I'd ever heard. "I figured you would be comin' to town after the storm. Just about everybody's here."

"Yes, I came to get some provisions. Why can't I come 'round to the store?"

"Whatcha need? I can get Nancy to fetch it," said Norman without answering the question.

Camille looked from wife to husband and back again. Her face was unconvinced and confused, a strange look on a woman like her. I could see her trying to understand the situation as she went along. Perhaps she was getting a taste of what I felt every day.

"Alrighty. Hi there, Nancy. I 'spose we could get along if we had some flour, sugar, coffee, and eggs. Jerky be nice too if you got it to spare."

"I'll be right back," said Nancy as she hurried away from us and down a grid of back alleys that smelled too much like urine.

"Okay, you are goin' to tell me what's goin' on. This place is about to explode. What happened, Norman?"

He looked up at me. The distinct glint of fear was in his eyes. Beads of sweat formed along his brow. Shaking hands mopped it away with a dirty handkerchief.

"Oh Camille, it just ain't safe for you."

"Why? Had Elder Jones been talkin' about us again?"

"No, it ain't him this time. The DRS came a few days ago. Bought up all the cattle from the ranchers. Even John Gibbons' herd."

"The DRS?" I asked feeling like I was already falling behind.

"It's the Drought Relief Service. The government funds it," provided Camille. "But I don't understand. That should be a good thing. John Gibbons ain't been able to sell those beasts in forever. They were nearly starving."

"They were. And yes, at first it was a good thing. The DRS folks came and paid for the lot of the cattle, but then they slaughtered nearly half of them right in front of the Gibbons family. Tossed the carcasses in a pit."

"Why would they do that?"

"Said it was the law. They took the healthier ones and dubbed the others below standard. John said it was somethin' about supply and demand and bureaucrats. Gonna take the good ones for processin' to feed the hungry. But those hungry Gibbons kids watched it. There's eleven of them, mostly skin and bones. They watched the federal men kill the cows and dump them in the ditch. All that meat wasted. I'm sure they hadn't had a decent meal in forever."

"What sort of help is that? Why couldn't they let the families get what meat they could off the carcasses?"

"John says it were a bunch stupid rules. The government bought them, the government said they were unfit. No one was allowed to eat unfit meat. DRS posted men with shotguns to shoot anyone who tried to get at the food. It weren't just that family. Lots of families are going hungry, and seein' your children watch a banquet rot in the sun can turn a man mean."

"But the meat they saved was supposed to go to the poor families. Did they give any back?" asked Camille just as bewildered by this story as I was.

"No. Said it had to be processed properly and then would be brought back 'round in those DRS trucks. Thing is we ain't seen one of them in months. Just don't make sense takin' food out of children's mouths like that for no real reason at all," said Norman.

"Never underestimate the ignorance of a pencil pusher followin' the rules to the letter. Most ain't got sense God gave a hat pin. But why are they mad at me? I had nothing to do with this?"

He looked up and down the alley in all its various paths as though worried someone might see them. Perhaps someone hid in the shadows, waiting to discover their meeting. Camille was unimpressed and unafraid with her shoulders thrown back, sunflower yellow dress billowing around her legs. She grabbed his shoulders, making him jump five inches high.

"Norman, stay with me here," said Camille trying steady the man.

"Sorry, sorry. Well, between that and the storm, it's a lot like them Frost children, Camille. I don't take no pleasure remindin' you of that, and I'm sorry, but that's what the whispers keep saying. Not to mention four more children showed up at the doctors with the brown pneumonia. Lungs practically caked with mud. And you just took on two new white children…"

"David and Delphia made a mistake, and it wasn't anything like this. They didn't hurt anyone. No one got sick," argued Camille.

Norman put up his hands as if to surrender.

"I know it ain't you. I know it ain't him or that Polly Jones neither," said Norman motioning to me with his eyes. "But they don't, Miss Camille. It's a powerful bad time to be thought a witch 'round here. Folks get crazy when their kids are hungry."

I wanted to say something, anything to defend Camille and make Norman understand we would be fine. This whole thing was so strange, it was hard to find sure footing in it all, but Camille was magical. She could do just about anything. We wouldn't be ousted like frightened rabbits. Camille could stop it all.

It was when I saw Camille's face that I stopped my huff. My mouth had opened to protest, but she looked up at me with this fear. I had seen this very woman stand tall against a white man far larger than her. She wouldn't back down in defense of a girl she barely knew. Now, she looked smaller somehow, resolved in the worst possible way. Standing up to one white man was one thing. Perhaps standing up to a whole mob of them was another.

Nancy came running down the alley to us, a gunny sack of goods in one hand and a crate of eggs in the other. I hopped down to help load the supplies, and she smiled at me with a smile warmer than the sun. It hid a fear behind it only easily seen in the sunlight.

"Here you go, Camille. We ain't got no jerky to spare, but I gave you some extra eggs," she said while handing the goods over to me to load.

Without meaning to, I thought of those words Camille told me when we first met. Ain't and no cancel each other out because they were both negative. It made a positive. Did that mean they *did* have spare jerky? Strange thoughts floated around when the world felt wrong. I wondered at the truth in the woman's words all the same.

Camille paid the money to Norman, and he took it gratefully. I reckoned there weren't many folks around here that could pay in hard money. Perhaps that was the source of the man's loyalty? After examining the glances between them, I decided no, it wasn't that. Norman may be skittish, but something else was behind this. There was a caring between the three of them, like something bigger joined kept them bound. It was a hard thing to place a finger on with no one telling me the story, but he was sweating bullets worried about Camille as well as his family. It wasn't merely money. Even Nancy reached out to clutch Camille's hand before we pulled ourselves onto the wagon. They shared a tender look and released one another.

I took my place, and Camille collected the reins. Before she clicked at Johnny Sanders to go, she reached under the seat and pulled out a very small sack. It was cheesecloth tied into a bundle with yellow ribbon. The sachet was foreign to me. I'd never seen her with it.

"Here Nancy, take this," said Camille as she tossed the little bag to her.

Nancy caught with a reverence in her face I didn't understand. She looked at the gift as though it were pure gold in her hands.

"Give it to the doc," said Camille. "Tell him to give it to those poor kids with the brown flu. Should help 'em."

"He'll never accept it," replied Nancy with tears in her eyes. "I'll try but if he knows it's from you, he'll…"

"Don't tell him it's from me."

"Then who?"

"Make up a story. I don't care. Some Indian medicine man came through or whatever. If it will save those kids, I don't care where he thinks he got it."

Norman nodded to her and pulled his wife tight in a hug. There were genuine tears in Nancy's eyes as we drove away. I waited until we were clear out of earshot of the town before I asked about it. Camille knew I would, and she cut me off before I got a chance.

"Cough drops," she said flatly as my mouth opened.

"What?"

"That's what you were going to ask me, and I'm telling you. They were cough drops."

"They had to be more than that. That Nancy lady acted like you gave a sack of jewels."

"One person's jewels are another person's cough drops. But you're right, Galahad, those were more than that. A bit of old magic Nan taught me."

"What sort of old magic?" I asked.

"Very old magic. The kind long ago of herbs and such. They are made of honey, peppermint, eucalyptus and the like. A few stranger things of course or else it wouldn't be very good magic. Nancy and Norman had a girl a while back who got the brown pneumonia. Poor thing already had a tough time of it with her breathing. She was the first to come down with it in town."

"She died?"

"No, she didn't. I came to them and offered my help. Gave them enough of these things to last a week. Told them to have her suck on 'em day and night. By the time the week was over, she was right as rain and breathing easy again. I convinced them to send her north to live with an aunt until the worst of this had passed. I brought her back once, but with her lungs, it might be worse next time."

Things were all starting to make a lot more sense to me. The tender looks, the fear for Camille's safety. It was all making sense.

"So, you saved their daughter, and that's why they're so loyal to you?" I asked.

Camille smiled and snickered a little. Johnny Sanders clopped along at a steady pace down the worn road. She followed him with her gaze as though not looking at much of anything at all.

"Well, I would hope they are loyal for the same reason I'm loyal to them. We are friends. The thing with their little girl may have started the whole thing to be sure, but it's nice to call them friends. I always hoped they felt the same about me. Not indebted."

Her use of the word 'indebted' sparked something inside me. A new knowledge about the tale she wove that seemed so small but meant so much more.

"They didn't pay you anything, did they? You did it without payment. Just like that doctor and those kids will never pay you back. They'll never even know."

"Sometimes it's best that way."

"Folks should know. All those people walk around making faces at you, thinking horrible things about you. They don't even know about all this good you're doing. We should tell them."

Camille merely waved her hand at me, dismissing my ardor.

"I only want one thing from folks. Just be kindly to one another. This cruel world we live in would be a lot more tolerable if everyone would just remember we are all people. Kindness doesn't seek reward, and neither do I."

CHAPTER EIGHTEEN

Calm descended upon the house like a gentle mist everyone invited. We breathed it in and held it in our lungs. It was clean and cleansing. Rain smelled this way if it every rained again. There was no guarantee it would stay no matter how much we wanted it to, so we held it in as long as we could.

I would venture to say we held our breaths a lot in the days that followed our brief peace. After a spell, we all started waiting for the other foot to drop, suspecting the quiet was merely a time the townsfolk needed to organize a mob against us. Every snap of a branch manifested ghosts of angry farmers marching on our home. The slam of the front door sounded like a gunshot in our ears. It was like sleeping in the boxcars all over again except here there was a hope we'd be safe, even if it was a false one.

My first effort to fight the tension led me to the garden. Camille had managed to revive the garden from its dusty burial, but with its resurrection came the weeds. I supposed weeds were about the only thing I'd ever seen that nothing could stop. Each one had to be pulled up by the roots, or else two would take its place.

So I dug in and weeded best I could. After hours of toiling, I had a pile of roots and a sore back to show for it. I stretched and threw my work gloves to the ground. The sight of those worn gloves on top of a stack of weeds brought my mind to Nan. When I first came to this place I had feared her above all others, and at that moment, she was the only person I wanted to see.

I rinsed my face and arms with the water bucket near our invisible windmill. After I was clean enough for presentation, I made my way to the house and straight on back to the library. Nan was there just as I hoped she would be. My heart sank when I saw she was sleeping. The old woman in her layers of clothing dozed in an oversized armchair, her gloved hands wrapped around a golden book. The gloves were red velvet this time with intricate gold filament.

What I wanted was a word, maybe a few of them if she could spare them, to make me feel better. Everyone was antsy, but I felt more listless than most. I stared down at the old woman, her body rising gently with every breath, and knew I couldn't wake her. That would be cruel.

Instead, I walked to the bookshelf and took a purple one from its place. Might as well try my luck, I reckoned. When I opened the book, there was no title, no words to speak of. Another blank book in my hand. Never had I felt so utterly lost and alone. To be so close to comfort and not be able to touch it. Perhaps going back to the weeds was my only good idea.

A floorboard creaked slightly behind me, and I turned expecting to see Nan rising from the chair. To my surprise it was Camille. She glided in the room, removing a sun hat and placing it on a nearby table. Nan continued to snooze in her chair.

"What are you doing in here, Galahad?"

"Just seein' if Nan was awake," I replied.

Camille smiled at me and sat on the window seat. She patted the cushion next to her and motioned for me to sit. I did so without hesitation even if I slumped over. Most of my energy had gone with the weeds.

"You like Nan, don't you?" she asked.

"Yes. She's kind to me. Not that you ain't. I didn't mean…"

Camille cut me off with the slightest shake of her head.

"Stop all that. I have enough of it with Polly, I can't stand a bunch of it from you too. Nan is comforting and kind. I agree with you. Let's leave it at that."

"Can I ask a question or is it rude?" I asked.

"Well," said Camille pretending to think about it. "I 'spose it depends on the question. That last one wasn't rude, so let's try your next one on for size. You always do have a lot of questions, Galahad."

"What I wanted to ask is about Nan. About the gloves."

"Why does she wear them?" provided Camille.

"Yes, that. Why?"

"Oh child, that's a long story."

"Forget I said anything. It's none of my business anyway," I blurted out.

"Now now. I didn't say I wouldn't tell you. I just said it's a long story. We got time for long stories right now, so settled yourself in and I'll tell it to you."

I leaned in closer, all senses at attention. I was happy to focus on something other than possible danger. Camille began her story in a gentle voice like a woman telling a fairytale. It wasn't like the story about Crow, fraught with pain and terror. Her face was smooth and gentle as though this story was about summer nights and lightning bugs. I relaxed into the smooth rhythm of her words.

"In the ancient times, there were different Gods. Primitive Gods of sky and dirt and blood. So many were they when a medicine man tried to count, they pried out his eyes with his own fingers. It was sport for them to play with him so. A mere mortal who tried to make sense of somethin' he didn't know."

"They played with humans? For sport?" I asked twisting my face in a sour way. Perhaps this wouldn't be such a nice story.

"To them, beauty lived everywhere but with humans. In the trees, the wind, the earth, and the heavens. People were frightened beasts who squabbled over resources even though the Gods gave them a bountiful world. Man was a terrible, violent creature, only interested in his own survival."

Camille trained her voice to be gentle again. She reached over and touched my hand. I waited for the "but then" part. Every fairytale starts that way. A world was one way, *but then* this happened, and it changed things forever.

"But then, they found somethin' that changed their minds. They found one person among the tribes. A child who was the epitome of good and kindness and beauty in the world. All of the Gods declared this child worthy of their love, but they had to leave their mark to protect it."

"Mark?"

"It wouldn't do to have such a child walkin' among the heathens of the world with no protection. No, not at all. Anyone could hurt them. So the Gods painted her with the brushes of the immortals. Her skin became a palette from the heavens. This made her immortal and powerful like them."

"So, she became a God," I said.

"Well, sort of. She was immortal for a very long time. But over the years, the Ancient Gods withered and faded away. New Gods took their place and forced what was left of the Ancient ones into the heavens to become stars in the sky. The Goddess child would go with them too, but they made a plan to save her. They would have to split her in two."

I stuck out my tongue and looked resolutely horrified.

"Not like that. They split her spirit in two. One part would be her as that innocent, mortal child she had once been, and the other would be the immortal goddess she had become. While she was always pulled toward the stars where the Ancient Gods went, the mortal child was there to anchor her to Earth. The two would be inseparable and immortal as long as they were together. If the child was killed, she would have no anchor. The tether would snap, and she'd float away. On the other hand, to touch a goddess would rub the immortal paint from her skin, and thus it would kill her and vanish the child who followed her."

It was a good story, I'd give Camille that much, but I was having a good bit of difficulty understanding how that applied to Nan and her gloves. My brow furrowed so much, a pain began throbbing in between my eyes. She could see my confusion, and Camille gave me a level look and nodded over to Nan, still sleeping peacefully in the armchair.

I gaped at her body, how old she seemed, and the gloves she always wore. My eyes grew wide when I realized I hadn't ever touched her, not her skin at least. For that matter, no one touched her, not even Camille. All those gloves. All those layers of fabric around her.

"Are you saying Nan's the goddess in the story? She was the child of kindness and light?"

"You didn't really think all this magic around was mine, did you?"

"Well, I guess not…but…a goddess?"

"After everything you've seen here, would that be so hard to believe?"

CHAPTER NINETEEN

Camille asked if I wanted any iced tea before she left me in the library. I declined the offer more in the effort to be alone than anything else. Despite my promise to Nan, there I was again trying to understand things that couldn't be understood. How could one wrap their mind around such things as old Gods and people painted with immortal brushes?

After Camille left me to my own thoughts, I crept over to Nan. She laid there. So peaceful in her dreams. I didn't want to wake her, but I had to get a closer look. Her gloved hands folded gently over her book. Nothing seemed powerful about them. I scanned all over her body and saw nothing but a nice, old woman who smelled of talcum powder and flowers.

I closed in on the only bit of skin visible on her, her face. My face closed the gap between us, leaving only a few inches between my nose and hers. I don't really know what I was looking for. Brush strokes maybe? Her clothes smelled like linseed oil.

The colors of her were the same as ever, plum in the dark bits and molasses in the lighter. Not the reddened scratch paper of my face or the dark honey velvet of Camille. Nan's was lovely and rich and full of lines that must have had a million stories behind them. Nothing looked like paint though. It was just skin.

"Didn't anybody ever tell you it ain't polite to stare?" whispered Nan.

I nearly jumped out of my skin. She had been asleep only minutes before. I was sure of that. Her breathing never changed. Now, I couldn't catch a breath to save my life. Nan slowly opened one eye and smiled at me.

"I got you good, didn't I?"

"Yes," I said still panting. "You did."

"Why are you spying on me, child?"

"I didn't mean to. Really. It was just Camille. She told me the story. The one about you."

"Which story about me? I've been alive a good long while. I reckon there's quite a few stories about me."

Her smile made me relax. My shoulders slipped down from around my ears, and I pulled up a chair next to her. Nothing in her expression said she might be cross with me. Nan even laughed a little.

"The one about the Gods and how they painted you," I said in awe.

"Oh Nat, I thought you had more sense than that."

"So, you're sayin it ain't true?" I asked not able to read her either way.

"Do I look like a Goddess to you," said Nan with a wry smile.

"But…but Camille…"

"Camille is a storyteller of the highest degree. She thinks she's real cute but doesn't fool me a bit. I 'spect she also told you about magical mosquitos in her pocket. My lands, that woman lives in a world of hyperbole."

I snickered, and she laughed along with me. I didn't know what hyperbole meant, but I caught the meaning of it all the same. The thing of it was she still wasn't answering the question one way or the other. Why did everyone in the house talk in riddles that answered nothing?

"What about the gloves?" I asked.

"Maybe I just like gloves. Things stay fashionable as long as no one else is around to tell you they're not. Besides, at my age, one's skin is as thin as paper. Better to stay fancy than look saggy."

Nan raised one gloved hand daintily in the air, flicking her wrist to and fro as though she were of high society. The golden accents glistened in the light as she moved here and there. She pulled a snobby face and used her other hand to push her nose into the air to a point.

"Quite frankly sir, gloves are a perfect accessory for any occasion," in a mocking accent.

We laughed again. She sounded exactly what I imagined the Queen of England sounded like, and it was fun to be happy for a time no matter how short. Then, a thought occurred to me. It didn't seem right in my brain, so I thought I might say it out loud to test it in the open. My Mamaw used to say sometimes you had to throw an idea against a wall to see what sticks.

"Is it Camille? Is she the Goddess in the story?"

"Heavens no. I told you how she came to me. Besides, you've touched her, haven't you? Held her hand? Grabbed things from her fingers?"

"Yes, but I don't understand…"

"What did I tell you about trying to understand everything? Sometimes you just have to let it be what it is. The understandin' will happen later. Don't force a thing into one of your boxes. You don't even know if it will fit. Best to let it pick out its own box."

"So…Camille made up everything. You aren't the Goddess," I said, trying to nail yogurt to a wall.

"Maybe I am. Maybe I ain't. A person can be so many things at once. Would you treat me different if I said yes or no? We are friends, and friends we'll stay whether I'm a Goddess, an old woman, or a rabbit in bull's clothing."

She patted me on the knee. The velvet of her gloves felt gentle and soft against my skin. I tried at that moment to go along with her, to understand how to *not* understand. Such an absurd way of learning. My mind rejected it every time. The idea was sandpaper against my skull, so I opted to change the subject to save myself the burn.

"What about those two," I said pointing at the photograph of the siblings with the light hair. "What were their abilities? Why aren't they here anymore?"

Nan's face went from playful to grim. Her mouth set in a hard line, a deep canyon on her face with river-like lines breaking away in the wrinkles.

"David and Delphia were special children. Camille found them in Amarillo working for a snake oil vendor. Man was as crooked as a politician and twice as mean. He was sellin' some concoction or another and using the children as entertainment."

My gut felt like it was falling downwards suddenly.

"What sort of entertainment?"

"Well, you see how they look. Right peculiar. He called them fairy folk. Dressed them up in leafy costumes and gave David a lute. The man adopted the worst Irish accent I ever heard. Sounded more like he was from the islands than Ireland."

"What did he have them do?"

"They whispered to the insects, you see. That was their ability. David and Delphia would summon butterflies, scores of them. They'd flutter about the children and land in their hair. People from all around came to see it. The crook sold fairy elixir from the fairy children themselves. Cured anythin' and everythin' that ailed you, or so he said."

"Was he their Daddy?"

"No. We never could find their parents. Who knows where he got those babies. Regardless, Camille saw what was happenin' and took them away from the man. Well, it was more like she took him away from them."

"She...killed him?"

"I don't think so. Hard to say. A tornado came through Amarillo that day. It harmed no shops and hurt no one. Nothin' was touched but the crook and his wagon. They were swept away down the road, never to be seen again."

"Camille did that? How can a person make a tornado?"

"You've seen for yourself, child. Do you really question it?"

I shook my head. Maybe I would have before what I saw her do in the storm, but not after. There were certain things you had to see to believe, and I believed whole heartily in Camille.

"But if she could do all that, why didn't she stop the storm altogether? She could have saved the farms, the town from all that damage," I said.

Nan shut her eyes and took a good while to open them again. When she did, it was with a groan and a little cough.

"This is somethin' you won't understand. I can tell you that fact right now. Not until you witness it in its entirety will you get this. I do love you child, but I know you. You will ask and ask and ask until we've talked all day. Even then, you won't get it."

"Please Nan. At least tell me what to look out for," I pleaded.

"I will tell you enough. It won't make much sense now, but someday it will," she said with a long sigh.

I felt bad for wearing Nan so thin, but I also had a mind desperate to know this secret of Camille's. Any answers would help me, I just knew it. If I had a better grasp on things, I could be more useful. The world might make more sense. I nodded to her a little too eagerly.

"Camille is more than she looks. You know that. You saw what she can do in the storm. Could she have changed that storm? Yes, more than likely, but she won't. She shouldn't. It's risky movin' so much that's natural. The act can swallow you up, change you. It can make a person lose themselves. People can get hurt when someone like Camille loses herself."

Nan looked older somehow and defeated. A dark shade flittered across her eyes as she stared past me to somewhere far away. Perhaps she was going back to another time, a memory where I couldn't follow.

"Is that what happened to the twins," I asked meekly next to her.

"Oh Lord, no. Camille loved those babies to the end of the world and back. David and Delphia were lovely children. Everyone adored them. It was hard not to. Never did I see a more innocent pair."

"What happened to them?"

Nan sighed and looked down into her gloved hands. The longing on her face made me hurt a little inside. I was suddenly very sorry I brought up any of this. It seemed no matter what I asked, it led us to dark places. The last thing I wanted was to hurt her further. She went on anyway. Apparently, even though it was a painful memory, Nan was going to revisit it for me.

"They spoke to bugs. Didn't even need a book to tell them how. It was just natural for them. When they came here, the books opened their knowledge to them without hesitation."

I took a self-pitying moment to direct my gaze at the bookcases. Rows and rows of special books. They had given their secrets to everyone but me it seemed. I swallowed the bit of jealous I'd been chewing and focused back on Nan.

"We figured out quickly they were special. Progressed quicker than any witches I'd seen. They advanced to more than bugs. Started talkin' to animals too. In fact, David's the reason we have ole Buck in the other room."

"I'll have you know that boy had nothing to do with my superb existence. He was merely a medium my exquisite soul used to grace this hovel with my presence," yelled Buck from the room next door.

"Oh yeah? Then where are your legs?" shouted Nan back at him.

"I don't need legs. With a face this divine, I don't need to be bothered with legs. Such a useless accessory."

"We both know you were some head Camille bought out the back side of a taxidermist wagon until David brought you to life. Now, shut your mouth so I can finish my story!"

"I will shut my mouth as long as you admit how positively exquisite my mouth is," said Buck.

Nan rolled her eyes as I suppressed a giggle.

"Fine, your mouth is exquisite. Truly, it is a sight to behold. Even royalty comes from miles around to gaze upon your beauty," replied Nan sarcastically.

"That's more like it. Go forth with your tale."

"As I was sayin'," said Nan a little louder for the benefit of Buck's ears. "David and Delphia were exceptional children. Truly. Camille doted on them as though they were hers. There was something' about those two. They had this innocence to them like the world was a lovely place where nothing bad ever happened."

"You mean, like Polly?"

"A bit, yes. Polly reminds me of Delphia a little. Probably one reason why Camille insisted on helping her. But Polly has lived some horrors. Not like you and not like me and not like Camille. We know the world and how it can be cruel. Polly knows a special brand of cruelty from her upbringin'. She may seem innocent in other ways, but Delphia was far worse off. It seemed that no matter what happened, the Frost kids saw only light and happiness."

"Well," I said after contemplating that. "That doesn't sound bad. I wish I ain't seen half the stuff I seen."

"True, but they didn't understand consequences. Without knowledge of bad outcomes, you can't think of consequences. One day, they wandered away from the house chattin' away with a group of rabbits. They had a warren on the property of another farm. The two spoke at length with the family of rabbits who told them of the mean farmer and his poisons. Somehow they convinced David and Delphia to play a joke on the farmer."

"How does a rabbit talk someone into doin' anything?" I asked.

"There you go trying to fit this into one of your boxes. They could coax an animal to talk, but there was no telling what that animal would say. Take Buck as an example," said Nan motioning in the direction of the cold study.

"I heard that, old woman!" shouted Buck.

She sneered at the doorway before turning her attention back to me.

"So, the Frost kids did it? The trick on the farmer?" I asked.

"Yes. They never thought it would lead to anything bad. To them, bad things didn't happen. So they whispered words into the breeze, callin' for the grasshoppers. And they came, oh boy, did they come. It was a blight on the farmland. Not just that plot but the others twenty miles in every direction."

I stared at her in astonishment. At first, I didn't know what to say. I'd seen blights on the rails. You'd look out the doorway as you passed farmland only to see withered crops or ones eaten away by insects. Mostly, folks blamed the lack of rain or terrible fortune. How might a community react when the culprit was a specific person, or rather, two people?

As if reading my thoughts, Nan continued on that idea.

"The community of Tanglewood was angry. Farmers live and die by their crops. Once word got out that two of Miss Camille's strange children could whisper to grasshoppers, we had a mob headin' our way. The folks 'round here already took umbrage to Camille harboring any white children at all, let alone strange ones. You better believe she would've gotten the brunt of their wrath."

"What happened? What did she do?"

"The hardest thing imaginable. There was no keeping those children here, no matter how much she loved them. Camille sent them with a friend down south to a convent. It was a place like this; nuns caring for children who were different. There was no town around. The convent had all it needed on its own, so there were no prying eyes. No townsfolk to disapprove. She knew David and Delphia would be safe there, but she cried for ages after they left."

"Why didn't Camille fight for them? She's so powerful. She made a tornado take a fella away. Who cares what a mob tried to do. Camille could handle it."

"You're right. She could," said Nan with a nod. "Camille could have summoned up a storm to kill everyone who crossed her path. But remember what I said earlier about losin' herself. When the mob came to her door, she bowed her head and told them she didn't know what happened to the children. They had run away."

I pictured the scene, angry farmers with pitchforks and torches storming the house. Smoke billowing up into the night's sky. Flames dancing in the eyes of every man in the crowd. It was hard to tell how much of it was my imagination and how much was added by books I read. Folks out to get the evil creature at the haunted house. But Camille wasn't a creature. She was a powerful witch. I just didn't understand why she wouldn't hurt them. Why did she roll over and send the kids away?

"I see your confusion, child. It's written all over your face," whispered Nan. "You'd be terrible at poker."

"I just don't get it."

"Think about it. Have you ever in your life been responsible for another person's sufferin'? Have you ever been the reason they hurt?"

Without effort, the scene in the last boxcar played in my head. The two fellows who tried to rob me of my boots. It was funny how I could recall their faces in perfect detail at that moment. The memory of Mamaw's face was beginning to blur in my mind, but the men in that boxcar were crystal clear. It was what the one man had said to me that made it stick, I reckoned. The curse that was his parting job.

This is on your head, son. If something happens to us. It's on you.

Yes, I had been the reason those men got hurt. For all I knew, the fall killed them. They tried to steal from me, and I had no choice, but there was a good bit of guilt in that.

"Yes, I have. I caused sufferin'."

"Then you know. Camille is like you. The valiant sort. One reason I think she likes you so much," said Nan with a wink.

"Yes, she calls me Galahad."

"You both like to protect. She hurt people while tryin' to save them. It weighs on a soul. She could have hurt that mob, those people. She could have kept her children and laid waste to the entire town if she wanted. There probably was a part of her that wanted to do just that. But think about the price on her soul. Think about the guilt she'd have to carry. Think of the families she'd break. No, she did what she had to do. She kept the peace. She kept the kids safe. She kept what really happens here hidden."

"Eventually though, it's gonna get out what really happens here," I said.

Nan laughed and patted my hand. From anyone else, the gesture might have seemed patronizing but not from Nan. It just felt warm and comforting like most of her was. I relaxed under her gentle smile.

"No one ever knows because they don't want to know. Rumors and stories to be sure. They whisper about us and watch from a distance, but no one ever really believes we are real. It's a funny sort of line. Trust me, child. I've lived here longer than I care to admit. I know."

"Just how long is that, Nan? I mean, how long have you lived here?" I asked, hoping my question wasn't rude.

"Oh, my dear boy. Wouldn't you like to know."

CHAPTER TWENTY

The snow flurry on the east side of the house had ceased for a while. The dust had buried it in a dune of silt, and the wetness from the snow mixed muddy. Besides, Camille said laying low meant no outside magic. We worried over the Australian roses poking up through the dirty slush that had collected from days of snow. The stalks were emerging through the caked mounds but not well, looking soggy and sick-like. Leaves drooped, and no buds appeared anywhere.

When it looked like we were about to lose the roses completely, Camille relented and started the snow cloud up again. In no time, the snow drifts were restored, and the air chilled that side of the house. The roses turned around nearly instantly, and we were all happier for it. No one so much so as Polly. She had taken a particular interest in the roses for one reason or another. When I asked her about it, her answer was a simple one. She really wanted to see a rose bloom.

"I never seen roses," she said with a smile. "Not real roses anyhow. There was a picture of one in a book I read, but I never seen a real rose. At the colony, things like that weren't allowed. Nothing was allowed to just be pretty."

The mention of reading reminded me of the growing library in my room. Like the books, other things began appearing. One night, I laid awake in my bed staring up at the ceiling. It was flat with wooden planks lined up horizontally going from the window to the door. Staring up at those planks, I remembered a conversation I had while riding the rails.

This old woman asked to share a car with me. There was plenty of room, and she was so feeble, I didn't mind her much. She could have been a skilled con woman, willing to rob me blind in the night, but I doubted it. I could hear a good deal of fluid in her lungs, and she needed help getting in and out of the car. Still, I sat on my bag just in case.

She said she was from Atlantic City. It was a city perched on a boardwalk overlooking the ocean. Hotels and the like just sitting above a beach on a roost of wood. I'd never even heard of such a place, but the way she described it, you just knew it had to be true.

"When I was younger, we moved up there," she said to me. "At first, it was little more than a town in the sand. A little oasis for folks like us. Then the big muckity mucks came with their bars and parties. Once they built up the boardwalks, everything changed. You could make a good bit of money during season and starve when it wasn't. There are two things I miss the most about that city. Candy by the ocean and the boardwalk. It separated two worlds; the rich world on top and the poor world below. Nice where things are that simple."

Looking up at my ceiling, I thought about what she told me. I tried to picture a world built on boardwalks, the ocean just below. What might the boards sound like when you walked over them? That candy she talked about. What did it taste like? I bet a bit like salt since it was next to an ocean and all. But then again, how would I know? I'd never even seen an ocean. Probably wouldn't either.

It was about that time, lost in my musings, I noticed a poster on my wall. It hadn't been there before. My walls were bare, yet there it was. It appeared just like the books. The city depicted in the poster was Atlantic City. Colorful illustrations of bathing beauties and ocean waves. A city of lights on a wooden throne. It looked like one of those advertisement posters you saw at the train stops.

More came later. Once, I was lying in bed dreaming of the orient. I had run into a sailor who told me he'd gone there. He was a nice enough fellow who gave me a dime to shine his shoes. Everything he said didn't seem possible, so I replayed the conversation back and forth again and again in my mind, trying to make sense of it.

Sure enough, another picture appeared on my wall. This one with pictures of a city I'd never heard of before. Taipei it was called. The buildings had roofs that curved upward in a way that didn't seem possible let alone practical. Golden tipped statues and tinkling pipe music. Strange dragons with hairy spines danced along the tops of buildings. It was so colorful it almost looked like the images were moving, writhing as they might in real life.

It went on this way for a while. I'd lay in bed and think of a place I'd never been. Something some person once told me about, or maybe a city I'd read about in a novel. Sure enough, a picture would appear on my wall or postcards stacked up on the dresser. London, Paris, Rome, Greece, New York, California. There got to be so many things, my room started looking like a travel agent's office. There wasn't enough wall space for it all. Some posters even started showing up on the ceiling. Looking at them made me smile like I was visiting the places myself. Some nights, I'd stay away and gaze at the posters on my ceiling, pretending I was a big muckity muck who was planning a trip to Atlantic City or Taipei.

One day, Polly and I were standing by the side of the house where it was snowing. The snow drifts had really begun piling up, and the roses were growing tall, little buds popping up here and there. We stood in short sleeves just out of the reach of the snow. Getting too close meant shivering, and those coats Camille had weren't fitting any better than they had before.

"It's gotten colder in there, don't you think?" Polly asked me.

"Yeah, the snow takes up more space too," I replied.

"I wish we could go play in it," she said while chewing her bottom lip; a gesture I found out to mean she was contemplating something. "Those jackets Camille gave us are so big I can hardly move in them, and all I got are these flimsy dresses. No pants or nothing warm."

A thought occurred to me. Our rooms had been bare. Camille said we'd fill them with what we liked. In my room, pictures of exotic places appeared when I thought about them. Maybe it would work with other things too…like clothes.

"Polly, have you noticed things showing up in your room? Things that weren't there before, and you know no one brought in? Maybe stuff you think about?"

"It's happening to you too?" she asked, looking at me surprised.

"Yeah. Posters of places I want to go or heard of. You?"

"Yeah yeah. Well, not posters like you, but other things. One night I wanted to see a waterfall. Not just see it though. I wanted to touch it. I saw this picture of a baby waterfall spillin' into a pond with big, pretty fish in it, and I thought how nice that must be to stick your toe inside a fish's world for a second."

"So, you got a picture of that in your room?" I asked.

"No. I got an actual waterfall! It's in the corner of my room and spills into this pretty little pond with three fish. Just like I imagined. I named them Ginger, Charlie, and Bonny."

"Really? You have to show me that."

"Come on then," she said dragging me away from the snow and back inside the house.

We gave a quick wave to Jacob in the kitchen before we raced through the hallway and into her room. The change in her room was breathtaking. The bare walls had been replaced with a delicate filigree wallpaper of blue and gold. It was reminiscent of the paper in Buck's room, the patterns I'd seen her admire before. My walls were still stark except for the travel posters. When Polly pointed to the back corner of her room, I saw it. A genuine waterfall.

There was a tangle of rocks and greenery jutting out from the wallpaper as if they'd broken through ages ago. A gentle flow of water came from somewhere inside the walls and flowed down into a small pond on the floor. Smooth river rocks lined the edged of the pond and separated a wholly impossible phenomenon from the very real floorboards.

Polly motioned for me to get closer. I peered inside, and there were three fish swimming around. The white and gold and red. So vibrant the colors didn't make any sense at all. When I touched the water, it was cool.

"How deep does this go?" I asked her.

"I don't know. I reached my hand down there and felt for a bottom but couldn't find one."

Polly gazed up at me, concern on her face.

"You look like you're thinkin' hard," she said pinching the skin between my eyes with her fingers. "Tryin' to understand again?"

"You've been talkin' to Nan."

"Yeah, I have. You ain't sore at me are you?"

"For talkin' to Nan?" I asked.

"No, well, yes that too. I meant the pond. If you want a pond, you can have one in your room. Just have to imagine it, right?"

"That's right," I said with a snicker. "And no, I ain't sore at you. It's a right pretty pond, Polly. More like I wish I was more creative. I thought my posters were neat, and then I came in here. You're much better at this than me."

"But you can too if you just…"

I put up a hand to stop her.

"It's alright. Not what I meant. I had this idea and wanted to see if it works. You wanna try with me?"

"Sure. What's the idea?" she asked, light filling up her eyes.

"Well, if these rooms give us the things we imagine, why can't we imagine new clothes? We could imagine thicker coats and pants and padded shoes. Ones that fit us. Then we could go play in the snow."

A wide grin spread from one of Polly's ears to the other. Her whole body tensed with excitement as she drew her arms together, pressing her forearms next to each other, and clapping her hands near her mouth.

"Yes yes! Quick Nat, you go to your room and try it, and I'll stay here. I think this will work!"

I got excited too, little nerves dancing around in my toes. I ran to my room across the hallway, and we both slammed our respective doors shut. Spinning around in my room covered in pictures, I didn't really know where to begin. There wasn't much of a protocol to this that I knew of. The other times it happened, I didn't think about doing it. It just sort of happened.

Looking around the room, I decided the dresser was the best place to start. If the clothes appeared, they'd do so there. I put my hands on the top of the dresser and concentrated hard on something to wear. The truth was, I'd never travelled anywhere that had a good bit of snow to it. I wasn't sure what to imagine.

There was a picture just above the dresser. I was almost eye level to it. It was one of the paintings in the room that didn't look like a travel poster. The painting wasn't glamorous like the others, showing pretty scenes with happy people. This one showed up while I was reading *War and Peace*. Well, while I was trying to read *War and Peace*. The book was a difficult one to tackle. The painting had several Russian and French soldiers fighting in a forest in the snow. The idea of so many soldiers fighting each other in the cold intrigued me, and I wondered what they might look like. A few minutes later the painting had appeared.

I focused on one of the soldiers. He trudged through the snow wearing a grey coat lined with brown fur. While his hat was a bit over the top, his coat, pants, and galoshes would suit. All I had to do was imagine them, so I shut my eyes and imagined the clothing, each piece of it individually.

When I opened my eyes, I pulled at the drawer to the dresser. Inside sat the exact coat, pants, and galoshes I'd seen in my mind. Brown fur lining and all.

I didn't waste time dressing my new clothes. It seemed odd pulling on winter clothing in the middle of a hot day, but nothing around this place ever worked the proper way. When I had finished dressing, I threw open the door to find Polly poised to knock on it.

She was dressed head to toe in fine white. Her coat was a white hide with white fur lining the inside and poking out of the collar and sleeves. Elegant red roses with swirling green vines trimmed the skirt and around her collar. The coat was so long, I couldn't tell what she was wearing underneath. All that showed through were her two small feet clad in white boots that matched her coat.

"What have you been reading?" I asked in amazement.

"What? Nothin' really other than my special book. Why?"

"You are just way more creative than me," I replied with a laugh. "Race you to the snowy side?"

"You're on!"

Instead of running down the hallway the way we came, Polly turned and ran back into her room. It was a confusing move at first, but when I saw her vanish through her bedroom wall, I knew her game.

"Cheater!" I shouted at her as I ran through the house.

Walls and rooms flashed past me as I raced through. I nearly slid into Jacob's table trying to redirect myself too late on the slippery kitchen floor. Beads of sweat were already building into wet rings in the fur lining of my coat. It was Texas in September after all.

By the time I rounded the corner. Polly was already there waiting on me. She had a mischievous grin on her face and a snowball in her hand. I took the few steps that meant the difference between the hot sun and frozen wonderland. The wetness at my neck seemed to freeze the second I did.

"Don't you dare throw…"

A snowball hit my face, decidedly ending my sentence. It was a burst of cold flecks, just the tiniest bit heavier than air. The cold of it stung my skin but in a pleasant way. When I wiped it away, my nose sucked in a breath, cold and clean smelling. Tiny remnants clung to the fur of my collar.

Polly laughed at me and pointed. I squatted in the snow, never taking my eyes off her, a telling grin on my face. I wadded up my own snowball and threw it at her. She tried to dodge it, but it exploded on her shoulder. Poll yelped when it hit.

"This means war!" she cried.

And war it became. The best war ever fought in the history of Tanglewood, Texas. We ran around lobbing snowballs at one another. Sometimes she hit me, sometimes I hit her. It was the laughing that was the real war. Who could make the other laugh the hardest? My stomach ached from it. Polly could barely draw in a good breath.

I fell at one point, and Polly practically snorted. She had to cover her nose with her mittens to cover the snot running down her nose. Her face, a combination of elation and embarrassment, sent me into stitches. I thought my ribs might crack from the sniggering and coughing. I bent over myself and fell again into a snow pile.

We were both cackling so hard, we could barely speak. It wasn't until Polly came over to me and tried to help me up that we saw Crow standing in his human form just outside the snowy line where summer topped, and winter began. Thankfully, this time he had clothes on.

"What are you doing?" he asked in all seriousness.

His stoic face looked reproachful, and we got to our feet like children caught with our hands in the cookie jar.

"We were just playing in the snow," said Polly cheerfully. "You wanna join us?"

Crow looked at her like she grew another head.

"Why?"

"It's fun," I said.

Crow looked doubtful and crossed his arms over his chest.

"It looks cold. I have a message for Camille. She sent me to look into something in Amarillo. I saw. I should tell her what I found," he said.

I didn't see her do it, and it seemed Crow didn't either. Out of nowhere, a snowball flew across the seasonal divide and smashed against Crow's sour face. It exploded into thousands of tiny, sparkling pieces. Each one melted into the water before hitting the ground. Crow scowled and wiped the wetness from his face.

I froze and looked at Polly. She stood next to me, an anticipatory smile on her face. There was a dare in her eyes, and for a long moment, no one was sure what the other might do. My focus bounced back and forth from Polly to Crow, waiting for something to happen.

To my surprise, Crow walked calmly over to the line where the snow began, bent down, and pulled together a ball of it. I'm not sure what was more surprising, the fact that Crow threw a snowball at Polly or the slight grin he wore while doing it.

He pegged her right in the face, and after the initial shock, she laughed loudly through a mask of powder. I retaliated with a shot to Crow's chest, and he got me with one to the side of my head. Crow had to be freezing running around with only a shirt and trousers on, but it didn't seem to slow him down at all.

War was waged again, and this time, there were three warriors instead of two.

CHAPTER TWENTY ONE

I don't know if she heard us or not, but when Camille came outside, she had a blanket in her arms for Crow. She wore a huge grin with eyes sparkling in the sunlight. As soon as he saw Camille in her colorful splendor, he stopped to let her wrap him in the warmth of the blanket. Camille patted his back, the slightest glimmer of a tear in her eye.

"I'm so glad to see you, Crow honey. You were gone so long, I was a little worried. Thought you might've found you another witchy woman to tend to."

There was a laugh in her voice, but at the mention of his trip, the air around Crow changed. The cold suddenly got to him. He shivered under the blanket, goose flesh sprouting up all along his shoulders and arms. Camille's face grew concerned. Her brow pinched together as she took Crow by the shoulders and ushered him out of the snowy area.

"What's wrong, child?" she asked.

"I was gone long because I found something."

"Alrighty, out with it," she said with a flip in her voice.

"I do not want to tell you."

Polly and I edged closer, making sure to stay on the cold side of the line. We were still in winter coats after all.

"What's going on? You'd better tell me, Crow. Was there news from the convent down South? Oh Lord, David and Delphia…they aren't…are they?"

"No. No," said Crow, shaking his head emphatically.

"Well, then. What did Percy say?"

"He wasn't there. His wife was sick. It was not him, and it was not the Frost children."

"Well, if there's one thing I hate is a game of charades. Out with it already! This better be good, Crow. The anticipation is enough to make me knock the black off your feathers."

"It is the circus," he said while looking directly into her eyes.

A pregnant pause held all of us in a prison of lost words. There was some sort of understanding between the two of them over that one sentence I didn't get. When I checked in with Polly, she merely shrugged her shoulders. She didn't know either, but we were eager to find out what was happening.

"Are you sure it's the same one? The one with Vivian?"

"I am sure."

"How do you know?"

"You do not trust me, Camille?"

"I trust you saw what you saw. Just tell me exactly what that was. I'm runnin' to catch up to you. Did you see the actual circus? In town?"

"No. It was a poster. The circus will be in Amarillo tomorrow and the following day."

"I can't imagine the stupidity of that man to move his circuit so close to me. Are you sure it was the right one? What did the poster say?"

"It said *Ramblin' Jack's Fair of Wonders.*"

A good bit of the color drained from Camille's face. For the first time, she looked old, even a little haggard. She was always so vibrant, I never really questioned her age. Camille had a timeless sort of beauty. Now, she looked more like the ghost of the woman who had rescued us from the post in town.

"That's it. That's Vivian's circus. No doubt about it. We're goin' in the morning."

At that, Camille turned on her heel and marched away from us. Not one word was thrown our way as a form of explanation. She didn't even look back. Polly and I were left gawking like the open-mouthed fish in her waterfall pond.

When Camille vanished around the corner, Crow slumped into the blanket. His gaze fell to the earth, and he shook his head gently from side to side.

"This is bad. This is very bad."

"What's bad? What happened?" I asked him.

"Nothing happened yet, but it will. No getting away from it."

"What is this all about? Who is Vivian, and why does Camille care so much about a circus?"

When my mouth said the name "Vivian," I instinctively looked over to the blooming rose bush in the snow. *Vivian's Rose* Camille named it. The real name was something else, but she renamed it *Vivian's Rose.* There had to be a connection.

"It is not my story to tell. It is Camille's. I did not want to tell her this news at all. It will only mean trouble."

"Then, why did you?" asked Polly in the most innocent way possible. "Why didn't you just keep this a secret? She probably wouldn't have known."

Crow bowed his head, not wanting to meet our eyes.

"It was not my secret to keep."

CHAPTER TWENTY TWO

For the rest of the day, the house was in turmoil. Camille was our even keel, our safe harbor. She was the lighthouse amidst the stormy waves of this new world we found ourselves in. Now, Camille broke the waves and angered the wind. She moved from room to room in a whirlwind of energy and frustration, packing trunks and then unpacking them. Wrapping up food and then unwrapping it and throwing it into sacks.

Polly and I tried to help her at first, but there was nothing we could do. Every bit of help we offered frustrated her more. We were nothing but a bunch of cats around her feet.

"Children underfoot!" she'd yell as we leapt out of her way.

After a while, we gave up asking questions and trying to be helpful. It was making her face turn a heated maroon. Polly and I decided to stick to the corners and let Camille bluster herself out of steam. Crow figured out this strategy early. He never even entered the house, just loitered around the front door having silent conversations with Jacob using only their eyes. I had been getting so used to Jacob, I could almost tell what he was saying when he said nothing at all.

Jacob started slapping his hand on the table in front of him to get Camille's attention. She ignored him at first, but he continued. At one point, he tried to reach out and catch her colorful dress as she blew past him, but Camille was too fast, and Jacob couldn't leave the chair he was sitting in for whatever mystical reason no one told me about. It was the same chair he always sat in. He slept there, he ate there. I had never seen him leave it even to go to the outhouse. It was still a debate between Polly and me whether he went to the bathroom at all. All Jacob ever did was sit at the table and play chess.

Now, he desperately wanted Camille to look at him. So much so, he stuck one skinny leg and tripped her. She fell to the floor a heap of headscarves and sunflower dress. Polly made to go help her, but I grabbed her arm and held her back. There was nothing to do now. Camille had a head full of steam, and her top was going to blow.

"What do you think you're doing?" asked Camille when she stood back, a red face glaring at Jacob.

To his credit, Jacob didn't flinch a bit. He jutted out his chin the way I'd seen Camille herself do in front of her own adversity. She softened enough to compose herself.

"Alright Jacob, you got my attention. Next time send Nan instead of tripping me," she snapped scornfully. "What is it?"

Jacob put his hand on the black queen chess piece and moved her across the board to where the white queen and king were. While keeping his eyes trained on Camille, he knocked the black queen over. Camille sighed.

"I know it's dangerous," she began but stopped when Jacob stood the piece back up and knocked her over again.

"Checkmate, yes I know. Alone, I know. What about with Nat?"

Jacob reached for the white knight and moved that piece next to the black queen. He knocked her down again. Checkmate still.

"Okay, how about if I take Crow with me?"

He went for the black knight and placed him next to our little fellowship. Again, he knocked the queen down. Checkmate again.

"And if I bring Polly?"

He slid the white bishop next to the queen, but this time, the queen didn't get knocked down. She stayed up.

"Ah, see. There's a way," said Camille with a devilish grin on her face.

I felt Polly shiver a little next to me. Jacob slammed his hand down on the table again, pointing the danger on the board. His mouth was in a hard line of frustration. Camille didn't let up or back down.

"I know I know, but it's not checkmate, is it? See, there's a chance."

"Don't you be ugly to him, Camille Lavendou," said Nan's voice behind us.

We all turned around and saw the old woman standing in the doorway to the kitchen, her arms folded over her chest. I don't think I'd ever seen Nan with a scowl on her face before. Somehow that made me more nervous than Camille's agitated state.

"I'm not bein' ugly, Nan. I was just…"

"I know what you're doin'. Do you? Can you see yourself right now? You need to stop this second, and take a good hard look at what you're doin'."

Camille stood in the middle of the kitchen and regarded us all. She met our eyes, even Crow who was still looking at us from outside through the window. Her shoulders slumped like a child who suddenly felt guilty under the scrutiny of a parent. All of her fury hadn't gone away, but enough had to stop her whirlwind tirade.

"I'm sorry, everyone. Jacob, I'm really sorry. It's just Vivian, Nan. They're back in town, the circus I mean. I've got to get Vivian. I have to try."

"Honey, I know it's hard, but are you willin' to risk all these children? To subject them to the evil of that man for Vivian? You love her, but what if somethin' happens to them?"

"He has no real power," said Camille.

"He has the power of persuasion, and you know it. It's how he lured Vivian away from us in the first place years ago. Don't underestimate his hold on people."

Camille looked up, the darkness covering her eyes again. I grabbed for Polly's hand and squeezed it.

"He shouldn't underestimate mine," she said through gritted teeth.

Nan seemed unimpressed. Her head tilted to the side as she pulled a half smile.

"And what is it you're gonna do? Huh? Rage into town and kill everyone there just to find Vivian? You know there's consequences to that sort of thing. You know from the Frost children. You know you have no right to ask these children to put themselves at risk to help you on a fool's errand."

"I have to do something!" Camille exclaimed, angry tears rolling down her cheeks.

Nan hobbled the distance between them and wrapped a gloved arm around Camille's shoulder. She wept like I'd never seen her do. Her face was a mass of pain. The layers of scarfs that made up Nan's shoulder soaked up Camille's pain in a puddle of wetness. It hurt to see such a woman that way.

"I know," Camille said at last when the weeping slowed. "I know I can't ask them. I know it's not right. I'll go at it alone. I can't see Vivian pass us by and disappear again. I have to try. She's one of us. It's my burden not theirs."

"I'll go," said the small voice at my side.

When I turned, it was Polly speaking, a determined look on her face. Everyone looked at her in surprise, except Nan. She just smiled a little and let go of Camille.

"What? Polly, no, you don't have to," Camille said, seeming like her old self again. "I'm sorry about earlier…"

"I want to. You put yourself in danger for me. It's only fittin' I do it for you."

There was a small pause where Polly's words hung in the air. Then, as lovely words often do, they floated to the heavens where they belong. Something set inside me like a gear fitting into place at the thought of her words. No denying it now. Jacob's chess set never did lie.

"Me too," I added. "You wanna get this Vivian lady. I aim to help."

We jumped a little as the screen door slammed shut to the kitchen. There was Crow standing in the doorway, chin jutted out proudly. His eyes set firmly on Camille.

"We will all go, like the board says. To find Vivian and bring her back."

I was eternally grateful Camille used no words at that moment. Sometimes, gestures were so big, words only lessened the message. We all felt the shift in the room. Tears welled back up in Camille's eyes, but this time, they fell over a smile. It wasn't pain, it was gratitude. After all, that was far better medicine than any bit of anger.

No one said much of anything else as we packed the provisions the journey would need. Positive thinking being the lifeblood of the longshots, we made sure there was enough food and water for one extra on the way home, for Vivian. As the first morning light broke, our little rescue party loaded up the wagon behind Johnny Sanders and headed into the unknown. Camille was at the helm with me by her side at the bench. Polly sat among the goods in the back, and a sleek, black bird perched itself near her. A motley crew for an improbable mission.

CHAPTER TWENTY THREE

Ramblin' Jack's Fair of Wonders had set up camp just outside the city proper of Amarillo. I had once seen the spectacular tents of *The Ringling Brothers' Circus* from afar during my travels, not having nearly enough money to visit it in person. The closest I came was digging in their rubbish for the leftover fair food paying folks threw out.

Ramblin' Jack's was not half as beautiful and only a quarter of the size. It wasn't much more than a cluster of ragged tents painted different colors with some music and tired men pushing food carts. The colors of the tents and the costumes of the workers faded in patches under the sweltering Texas sun. His main attraction was a menagerie of large cats who were so uninterested in the people around their cages, they slept despite children tossing pebbles at their feet.

We arrived and boarded Johnny Sanders and his wagon in a large barn nearby. It was mostly empty save a few work horses. The pasture next to it was full of automobiles as it had become the preferred way to travel by those who could afford it. I reckoned the rest either walked or didn't come at all.

Camille paid our way in wearing the tamest dress I'd ever seen on her. It was maroon with grey trimming; a lovely combination on anyone else, but on Camille, it looked positively drab. A matching scarf wrapped her hair, and I watched as she lowered her eyes to the ticket taker, trying to hide the radiant thing she was. We were under the guise of ordinary patrons, so Camille tried her hardest not to stand out, not to be herself. I understood the ploy, but still, my heart ached to see it.

The three of us made our way into the circus, trying to blend in with the herd of regular folks. Farmers, ranchers, and store clerks brought their families to see the lackluster sights. So many families looked world-weary, so maybe the attractions were lovelier to them. The tents and performers drooped in the wind and faded in the sun, yet I continually heard passersby remark on how lovely everything was.

I tried to take it all in, but my eyes kept wandering to the sky. Crow followed us from there, flying from one tent pole to the next. Occasionally, he caught an updraft and circled high above everyone.

"How will we know where she is?" whispered Polly to Camille and me.

"Vivian will be hard to miss," Camille said back to her.

She sure wasn't. Out of the monotony of drab tents, a flower sprung forth. It was no different in size really, but the color of it was so entrancing. Pink walls with a gentle yellow canopy, like the kind buttercups left behind. There were no patches or oil stains. Just a pristine tent with the words scripted out in pretty purple.

Madame Vivian's Wonders

Camille took a deep breath. I regarded her as she eyed the sign. Her whole face was tense as if readying her body for the oncoming task. She grabbed our hands, and with a loud exhale, led us through the flap among the crowd.

Once inside, we filed in line with everyone else. There were some chairs in the center, but they were already taken with the elderly and infirmed. It was just as well. For our purposes, sticking to the outskirts would be better.

We stood along the back, lined up like sardines. A portly man next to me pulled out a tin of crab. While he worked the key down the tin, an overwhelming aroma of pickled shellfish wafted over us. Between that and the nerves, I was afraid I'd give up the mission and run outside to vomit.

A gasp rang out among the crowd. At first, I thought the other people had smelled the same horrid odor as me, but when I turned my nose back to the stage, I saw otherwise. Vivian, the Madame herself, stood completely still on the stage in front of everyone, a half smile on her face. She wore a light pink dress with a sky blue sash tied around her waist. Her hair was the color of copper, short and pinned into the place. Tattoos covered her arms from the shoulders to her wrists, looking black and harsh against her pale skin. There were angel pictures all over her, wearing the same half grin as she had. The stage had been empty one second, and then, she was there in all her splendor.

I felt Camille tense next to me. She squeezed my hand, never removing her eyes from Vivian's face. There was a longing there I'd ever only read about.

When the smell of the crab hit Vivian, we all could tell. Her nostril flared, and her face soured. The terrifying thing about the reaction was that the angels tattooed on her arms mimicked her expression. Each one looked exceedingly annoyed.

"I do declare, I have been accosted by a stench in this here tent," said Vivian with a southern belle accent so smooth it was coated in butter. "While I do hate bein' rude, I will ask the fellow in the back row to take his putrid snack outside as it is attacking my dainty sensibilities."

A few people giggled. I wanted to, but Camille was stiff as a board, and I didn't want to spook her any more than she already was. The man with the smelly tin looked properly embarrassed and skulked out of the tent.

"There, that's better," said Vivian, a lovely smile returning to her face. The angels on her arms followed suit to the collective gasping of everyone in the crowd. "I am so happy you came to see me on this fine day. May I introduce myself? I am Madame Vivian, and I am the third most wonderful being in this here tent. The first of course would be my angels. Blow them a kiss, girls."

On cue, the angels on her arms all animated to blow a kiss at the audience. There was a mixture of shocked gasps and nervous laughter.

"The second wonder, well..." began Vivian before she darted her eyes around the room. They stopped on Camille for a long second. Madame Vivian didn't leave them there, but she held them there long enough to let Camille know she saw her. Vivian quickly found an elderly lady in the second row and gestured to her. "Of course, the second wonder would be her. Such a beauty. More radiant than the sea at Christmas. Everyone give Lavinia here a hand."

Everyone clapped and giggled as Lavinia blushed under her greying skin. She looked around with more than just embarrassment though. It was quite amazing to see a person light up so quickly. I watched as she mumbled to the people next to her, "How did she know my name?"

"And that brings us to the third wonder, which is little ole me. I am Madame Vivian, ladies and gentlemen. Seer of the unseen, teller of fortunes, mystic of the Mississippi. Who among you has a question for me?"

A little girl stepped forward from her family. Her older brother stood behind her, poking her with his finger. He was about as old as Luke was, and I saw Polly set her jaw when the same connection fired in her mind.

"Miss...uh Miss..." tried the little girl.

"Madame Vivian, sweety. Try again. We are in no hurry," she said kindly.

"M...Madame Vivian. Where is my kitten? He ran away three days ago. Can't find him anywhere."

Vivian closed her eyes and placed both fingers to her temples. A low humming sound came from somewhere seemingly deep inside her. I wondered if this part was necessary or just theatrics. When she opened her eyes again, everyone nearly jumped with the suspense.

"You have a hayloft, yes? It's in your barn?" asked Vivian.

The little girl's eyes grew rounder.

"Yes. We do!"

"That's what I thought. The kitten is there."

The little girl turned around with a big smile, full of excitement.

"Daddy, let's go get him!"

"Hold on a second," said the older brother, stepping out next to his sister. His face was one of cruelty and malice. The swagger of a mind who think he's knows everything there is to know already. "That's not much of a wonder. I bet everyone here's got a hayloft in a barn. Sounds like a liar talkin' to me."

The girl's face fell, and I saw Polly press her lips together in a tight line. Luke would never have been so cruel to her. Personally, I wanted to walk over and sock the kid myself. Vivian was the only one who didn't seem moved by the boy at all.

"You require more proof, I take it?" asked Vivian sweetly.

"I think I do. That is if you can," he shot back.

His father reached for him with a rough hand, but Vivian waved him away.

"Think I've got this one if you don't mind, sir. I'm sure you get tired of whoopin' this one so much. I bet he's a holy terror at home."

There was a smattering of laughter. The boy crossed his arms over his chest with a pouting lip stuck out. He didn't back down though, and instead, stood out in the open for the next volley of arrows from Vivian's tongue.

"You see, dear Dillan," began Vivian. She paused to take note that Dillan's face fell the second she mentioned his name. "Yes, I do know your name is Dillan, but where was I? Oh yes, the kitten. The kitten is hiding in the hayloft. He's up there feeding on mice and stealing water from the cow troughs. He loves your sister dearly and wants to be with her, but he's too afraid of you. It seems young Dillan here has been taking to stealing his father's bird rifle and shooting at his sister's kitten. Your aim is just terrible, but that kitten ain't no fool. He's didn't stick around to wait for you to get better."

Dillan's jaw hung open. It would have been comical had everyone not been just as shocked. His little sister had her hands over her eyes, crying beneath them. Their mother reached forward and slapped Dillan on the back of the head so hard, it made his teeth clack together. A few people laughed.

"Don't worry, dear little Lisa. Your kitten is quite safe. Just go up to the hayloft, and you will see. He's going to be a great mouser. You'll see. Mom and Dad, maybe lock up those guns for now? I got me a good switch tree out back if you need to cut a branch down for the ride home."

This time the entire tent roared with laughter as Dillan's father grabbed him by the ear and marched him out of the room. His mother and sister were hot on their heels, but the little girl did pause for a second to thank Vivian and wave to everyone.

"You're welcome, child. Go cuddle that kitten! Now, who's next?"

We kept to ourselves and watched as Vivian bounced from one person to the next, solving their problems and answering their questions. It was uncanny. She seemed to know everyone's name and their innermost wishes. I couldn't see the con, no matter how hard I looked for it. This had to be magic, but what kind?

"How is she doing this?" I whispered to Camille.

"She's clairvoyant."

"What's that mean?"

"She sees what others don't. Mainly thoughts. She learned it at Nan's."

"And the tattoos that move?"

"Ink magic like the books. Now shush, so you don't give us away."

We watched her work her magic on another woman, telling her she needed to go to the doctor because she might just be pregnant with baby number three. Everyone whistled as the woman disappeared with a blush in her cheeks.

A man stood a few feet away from us with an earnest look on his face. His feet were set wide apart so as to not shift his weight much. Every time he raised his hand, with the other people wanting her to answer a question, and every time she called on someone else.

"Why won't she call on that fella?" whispered Polly.

"It don't take a clairvoyant to see he's trouble," whispered Camille. "She won't call him. Only stick to the light-hearted folks."

That was exactly what happened. The stocky man raised his hand, again and again, only to be ignored. When he removed his hat in frustration, the bald spot beneath glowed red with anger. I didn't know what his game was, but I was sure we didn't want any part of it. When he turned and spat a wad of chew on the dirt floor, Camille's breath caught inside her. His face was squat and uneven like someone squished the lower part of his features and stretched the top of his head away from his nose.

"Who is it, Camille?" Polly asked.

All that came out were three little words, but they were enough to let us know everything we needed to know. *Snake Oil Vendor*. The man who held the Frost children. The one who Camille swept away with a tornado. Had he come back to find them? Was that his question for Madame Vivian, the third wonder?

Camille stepped gently backwards into the shadow of a tall man nearby. Without a word, Polly and I moved in front of her. He didn't know us, but he knew Camille for sure. If he made us, the entire rescue mission would be ruined.

Luckily, Vivian never called on him. She entertained the crowd around her, bringing to light only happy facts, fanciful things. One man wanted to know where his no-account brother hid his coin collection when they were thirteen. Another asked about his mother's will. A woman asked about rain and when it might come to their farms. Vivian predicted there would be a big rainstorm in two days' time. This got tremendous applause.

All this time, the stocky man with his hat in hand tried for her attention, but he never got it. After the cheer went up about the rain coming, he gave up and stormed out of the tent. I guess he reckoned the show would end on that note, a high one. He never so much as looked our way, and Camille was able to come out of the shadows as soon as he left.

"Thank you, everyone!" shouted Vivian over the applause. "I sincerely thank you for your attendance today. Please do enjoy everything our fair has to offer. And don't forget to put those buckets out for the rain comin' in two days!"

Everyone clapped again as they began to file out. There was a sudden urgency for everyone to exit. The tent had become stuffy with humans living and breathing so close to one another without a breeze to break up the moisture. We kept to the back wall as the people made their way out in lines around us.

As soon as the last patron left and the tent flap slammed shut, Vivian leapt down from the stage and hurried over to Camille. They ran at one another and embraced in the middle of the tent. It was the way actors did on the moving picture shows. The two women threw their arms around each other. Camille cried in the embrace as did the angels on Vivian's exposed arms. They even kissed right in front of us. So intimate was this moment, Polly and I felt like we had to turn away. It seemed too private to witness first hand.

"You shouldn't have come, Cammy. It's so dangerous."

"I had too, Vivian. I just had to."

Chapter Twenty Four

"He's going to kill you," said Vivian as she pulled away.

"Let him try," said Camille darkly.

"No, you know how he is. He's got everyone at the circus working under his spell. They'll do just about anything he says."

"Persuasion like that only lasts so long. You know that. It wears off."

"I know, but it can work if he gets his hooks in you. It did with me. By the time I was able to pull away, it was too late. I was already pregnant," said Vivian with tears in her eyes.

"Pregnant? You had a baby?"

"*His* baby. Jack Jr., I had to stay after that. Don't you see? He said he'd hurt baby Jack if I ever left. That's why you gotta go before he does somethin' terrible."

Camille looked around the tent frantically as if the solution was running around the dirt floor somewhere. Maybe her vision was going sideways. I was getting dizzy from the story myself, and I was only listening to it.

"Where is he? The baby?" asked Camille.

"He's asleep in my tent. One of the girls watches him when I'm workin'."

"That's good. We'll go get baby Jack and then get the both of you out of here."

"But Cammy, Jack won't let…"

That shadowy darkness covered Camille's eyes once again. A seriousness coated her tongue with molasses so every word that came out was dark and stout and true.

"I'd like to see him try," said Camille.

Even I shuddered under the weight of what Camille said, and I was on her side. Something about it snapped Vivian out of her frightened loop and put a light of hopefulness inside her pansy blue eyes. Camille took her hand, and I took Polly's. We made our way out of the tent as a hopeful team only to be stopped by the inevitable truth waiting for us outside.

The stocky man from the show stood next to a lanky fellow holding a baby on his hip. The baby had to be only a year old at the very most. A shock of copper hair in a little tuft on the top of his head made no mistake the child was Jack Jr. With the same hair on his head, Jack Sr. stood next to the stocky man with a terrible grin on his face. A group of men lined up behind him as if beckoned to.

Polly and I were still as could be. Camille held on to Vivian's arm, trying to steady her. The poor woman shook all over, her angels screaming in silence.

"Well well," said Jack slowly. "I 'spose we have us a little reunion of sorts."

There was a tiny voice in my head that wasn't there before. It poked around and whispered things to me, things I didn't agree with, things I'd never agree with.

"You don't owe that darky nuthin' at all," it said in my ear. "This ain't your fight. Just walk away now."

I looked around me but saw no one. Just Polly who was shaking her head back and forth as if she heard it too. Horrible voices saying horrible things. It hurt the more and more I heard their words.

"Take your girl and run far away from here. Do it while you still can," it whispered again.

Polly had her hands over her ears now, trying to block out the voice. In a rush of understanding, I knew where it came from. Jack. It came from Jack. When they talked about the power of persuasion, that's what they meant. He had the ability to whisper things in peoples' minds to persuade them to do what he wanted.

When I looked back at Jack, he was still smiling at us, watching Polly and I dance under his strings like puppets. Polly was getting violent, slapping her hands against her forehead. Why it wasn't hurting me like that, I didn't know, but something had to give. I pressed the little voice down down down. I couldn't get him out completely, but he was muffled at the very least.

"Jack, you stop hurting these children!" yelled Vivian.

"Oh sugar pie, you can see for yourself I'm not hurting anyone. I'm way over here. It ain't my fault that yet again Camille Lavendou has taken two mentally disturbed children into her care. Another set of white ones at that."

"Yeah," said the stocky man next to him. "That's the one. The darky that stole my children. I've been lookin' fer you."

He pointed a knobby finger at Camille. Her gaze hardened as she looked at

Jack's smug face. No fear was left in her. Nothing lived there except rage.

"Come on back to me now, Viv baby. Little Jack Jr. needs his mama," said Jack in a slithery voice as he beckoned her with one hand.

"She's coming with me," said Camille. "Give her the baby, and we'll be on our way home."

"Oh, is that what you think," Jack said laughing. "Even if I let you leave here, how were you planning to get out of town? I spied that ragged old mule the second I saw him in the barn. Locked the thing up tight, so you ain't goin' nowhere."

More people lined up behind him, lured in by his little voice of persuasion. Many were not carnival workers. Even farmers and passersby were lured into the spectacle. Camille released Vivian's arms as his number grew to ten times what we had.

"I'm sorry," Vivian said to Camille with tears in her eyes. "I have to go back. He's got my baby, Cam. I can't leave him."

Camille nodded to her, never taking her eyes away from Jack's terrible grin.

"You get that baby, Vivian," she said evenly.

"Please Cammy, run."

"Just go get the baby."

Vivian let go of Camille and closed the distance of the no man's land to where her husband and child were. She gathered the boy in her arms as Jack pushed her just behind him. I could see her whispering in his little ears something, but I couldn't tell what she said. The other people behind Jack were getting restless, especially the stocky man. A vibration rippled among them. It was angry and violent. The angels on Vivian's arms looked terrified.

"Camille?" I asked.

"Nat, you get Polly and leave," she said evenly.

"What? No."

"Get Polly and leave me here. It ain't your fight."

"Let's teach her a lesson!" screamed one man.

"A darky who don't know her place!" hollered a lady in the back.

"She stole my children!" yelled the stocky man.

There was a rumbling on the ground that rose and fell in a rhythm. Feet stomped to it. Picks and shovels struck the earth to it. It got louder, banging again and again in an ever-quickening beat. The mob behind Jack beat their war drums to the tap of his toe. Somewhere deep down, a voice told me to move or die.

I went to Polly. She was on her knees in the dirt now, holding her ears. Kneeling down, I grabbed her hands away from her head.

"Poll, get up. Push his voice out of your head. You're stronger than him. Remember how strong you are. Remember you're a witch."

Polly blinked up at me a couple of times. She swallowed hard as she focused in on my eyes. The strain seemed to ebb. I hoped that meant she was back in control of herself, even if only a little. A little would be all she needed to get away. Crow flew down to us and landed on Polly's shoulder. Whatever fog was left in her mind seemed to fade away under his touch. I helped her stand up.

"Can you move other things through walls?" I asked her amidst the cacophony of the mob's rhythmic threat.

"I…I can try," she said.

"Go now, take Crow. Run. Get the wagon and Johnny Sanders. Come back for us. Go!"

Crow leapt into the air and flew away from us toward the barn. Polly took off after him, trying to wipe her tears away as she went. The crowd let them pass with little more than wry laughter from their leader.

"Good move, kid. Good move," he shouted after her. Jack turned his smug nose back to Camille. "Best send the boy along too, Camille. No need for him to get hurt."

"That's one thing we can agree on," said Camille through gritted teeth. "Go on, Nat. Go after Polly. This ain't your fight, Galahad."

I stood up tall as I could manage and stepped in front of Camille. If a man stood a few paces in front of her, he'd block any direct line they had no matter his size. It may not stop a mob, but it would block a bullet, and that's all I had to give.

"It *is* my fight. You men and women will go on now. You don't really want to be here. He's making you, persuadin' you with his words. This woman has done nothin' to any of you. Walk away from this."

"She took my children!" yelled the stocky man, red-faced and shaking from the anger.

"No, she didn't. They weren't yours. They left with her on their own," I said.

"You don't know!" he screamed.

"I do because I left with her too. She takes in children who need homes.

That's all. She's a kind woman who cares for us. Shame on you all. Just look at yourselves. A group of twenty people out for the blood of one woman and the children she cares for. What sort of folks are you anyhow?"

The rhythm of the mob stopped. No more heavy breathing, no more grinding of teeth. Folks shook their heads and looked around at one another as if wondering how they got there and why they had been riled up at all. Several groups scattered away, seemingly unaware they were nearly a part of a murdering party. Even the circus folk shook their heads and stuck their fingers in their ears. Only the stocky man remained angry. For his part, Jack just stared at me amused.

"That's a neat trick, kid," he said with a chuckle. "You teach him that, Camille?"

"No Jack, don't you do it!"

It was Vivian who screamed and reached for his arm, the baby still perched on her hip. Her good intentions were too late. As effortlessly as if he were scratching an itch, Jack pulled a small pistol from the waistband of his pants and pointed it squarely at my chest.

In a flash, I knew it was all over. My brief time on this earth would end here. At least it would be a good death, one defending my friends. That's really all a person could hope for in life. Be loved and love others. Have a good death where you tried to do right by the folks in your life. There were worse ways to go. After all, I had once grown roses in the snow with a pretty girl. How many folks could say that?

CHAPTER TWENTY FIVE

I heard the gunfire and the muzzle flash. The pain would come shortly, I just knew it. Funny, no matter what I told myself, this really wasn't the way I had expected to die. Murdered in a boxcar maybe. Taken over by a fever in some back alley. Shot among witches in a cut-rate circus was an unexpected way to meet the grim reaper.

Time froze, at least, I thought it did. I kept waiting for the pain of the bullet, but nothing came to me. The idea he missed wiggled in my brain, but the man stood in front of me. Still, his barrel pointed to my chest. He had me dead to rights. Only a complete fool would miss at this range. Still, nothing happened.

It wasn't until I saw the frozen surprise in their eyes grow that I understood time had not stood still. I was not dead, not even wounded. Jack himself lowered his gun to stare at me. No, he didn't stare at me. He was staring at a small bullet on the ground about a foot in front of me. Somehow, he missed.

"The hell with this," he said firing his gun three more times.

Each bullet whirled toward me and slammed itself against a barrier even I couldn't see. They bounced off and pinged on the ground next to their comrades. I was in a bubble, one like the day of the dust storm. Just like the one Camille had made for me then.

I turned around just in time Camille standing still and angry beyond anything I'd seen in her. Her stance was steady, her feet like roots in the earth below. Camille's hands were at hip level, finger stretched out and tense. Above her, the sky roared with all the rage she had inside her. What had been a blue sky only seconds ago, moved and swirled into a tumult of anger above her. The clouds turned grey then black then tinges of green. A funnel spun together and dipped in and out of the heavens above her head. Her words carried with a raging wind and a crash of thunder.

"You dare try to hurt my child?" said the voice inside Camille's throat.

It echoed like in a storm so much it barely sounded like her voice at all. The sky rumbled around us, lightning flashing like spidery fingers along the belly of the clouds. Again and again, Camille's wrath pulled the storm to her. The clouds became her skin, the lightning her spidery veins, the booming thunder the sound of her voice.

People scattered, running for their lives. What few followers were left went running the second Camille called upon the thunder. Everyone ran to take shelter in any place they could. More frightening than the storm was Camille's stillness in it. Her control of something so beastly. While her body was still, her anger filled the air, turning it wet with rage.

The rain poured down on everyone, except Vivian and me. We were in our own protective bubbles. She held her baby tightly to her chest while Jack turned around frantically yelling at his followers. In the distance, I saw an even more peculiar thing. An ornery mule ran out of the barn with a wagon hitched behind it. This in itself wouldn't have been that odd had the door been open, but the mule pulled the wagon through the locked door of the barn. Polly sat on the bench seat next to a naked Indian boy who held the reins. She had done it.

I knew there wasn't much time left. The confusion wouldn't hold out. I ran full boar at Jack in his befuddlement and punched him as hard as I could in the nose. Pain seared through my knuckles, but my heart was pumping, so I swallowed it down. Besides, I had felt a snap on his part, and when I pulled away, blood was streaming from his face and mixing with the rain. He drew back and landed on his rear.

Vivian was at my side as soon as I whirled around. I grabbed her hand, and we ran back to Camille. Our bubbles were gone, and the wind and rain pelted us until we made it to the wagon parked behind the angry witch. Vivian handed little Jack Jr. to Polly. The boy child's wails were drowned out in the roar around us. Polly threw a blanket around his little-wet body as Crow, and I helped Vivian in the back. She wedged her body in between two sacks and cradled Jack Jr. there with her.

Crow threw a blanket around himself and jumped back into his spot in the driver's position He yelled at Camille to get in. Camille didn't get in the wagon; she didn't even turn.

"Camille!" Polly yelled. "Let's go!"

No response. Nothing at all. It was as if she wasn't here anymore.

Lightning struck the ground near the circus. Every time it did, there was a loud bang and an explosion of soil and grass. All around us, the air was hot with electricity. The twister forming above Camille grew wider and wider above her; the base slowly being pulled to the earth by some invisible tether Camille seemed to hold.

Women screamed, children wailed, and still, Camille didn't relent. Her gaze was fixed on a point in front of her. She was becoming the storm, and the storm was engulfing her, and all that fury followed her fixation.

When I ran to her, she didn't even see me. All she could see, all she wanted to see, was Jack. He cowered yards away from her, pelted by rain and shivering under the bloody nose I had given him. Even Vivian's baby crying didn't move the witch. Everything was going too far. Camille would lose herself to this storm's rage if I didn't stop her.

"Camille!" I screamed in her ear.

She ignored me. The funnel descended lower and lower. The sound following it was so familiar to me. It was the sound of a freight train roaring past.

"Camille, stop it!" I yelled again.

Still, she ignored me. I couldn't let her do this. I couldn't let this rage sweep her away with it. This was all my fault.

I slapped her across the face out of sheer desperation. It wasn't a hard slap, but it was enough to sting the knuckles I hurt on Jack's face. Camille turned and looked me in the eyes, finally seeing me in focus. I put my hands on her shoulders, and she blinked several times at me.

"That's enough. Please, Camille. It has to be enough now. We don't want to lose you."

Camille's tension eased out of her slowly, and as it left her so did the storm. The twister retracted back up into the sky and dissipated among the clouds. The rain ceased pouring, and the heavens went silent. With one last deep breath, Camille returned to us, and the rage in the air was silenced.

She was Camille Lavendou once more. The version of Camille who could see us. Her hand went over her chest as she breathed in and out in heavy gasps. Beads of salty sweat rolled down her face to blend in with the rain she had commanded.

"Thank you, Galahad," was all she said as she took my hand and ran with me to the wagon.

Crow and I helped her into the driver's seat. Camille was always strong, but this time her solid posture wobbled a little. Nevertheless, she had Johnny Sanders racing away from the circus as fast as his stubborn hide would take him. He kicked up mud everywhere as we tore through it. I looked back to see Jack trying to stumble after us with blood still streaming from the broken nose I gave him. The madman raised his fists to the heavens.

"Damn you, Camille! I know you made enemies. You best bet on seeing me soon! You hear that, Vivian? We'll be coming for you all real soon!"

CHAPTER TWENTY SIX

Never had I ridden so long and so quietly in all my life. Every word not spoken between us was worse than if we were all alone. No one spoke. Jack Jr. barely cried. It was as if the child himself sensed the gravity of the situation and decided to keep silent. At one point, Polly wept to herself, curled up in one corner of the wagon with her knees pulled to her chest. I wanted to crawl back there from my post riding shotgun to comfort her, but Crow got to her first. He had a blanket wrapped around him, and he shared it with Polly as she rested her head against his chest.

There was no denying the small pang of jealousy in watching that, but there were more pressing matters to deal with. Still, it was there. Everyone in the wagon was special. Everyone had their person to comfort or be comforted by. Everyone had some great gift that helped to save us, except me. I was adept at being brave and comforting. Now, the only thing I was good for was taken by someone else. It stung.

Camille drove the wagon, stoic and unmoving. She said nothing, barely looking at anyone else. The only words she uttered the entire drive were said about two miles out of town.

"Trouble is comin'. I'll understand if you don't want any part of it, Viv. It's comin' for me no matter what, but we could drop you and Jack Jr. somewhere safe. I can put you two on a train set south to where the David and Delphia are. You'd be safe."

Vivian shook her head slowly. The baby had fallen asleep by that point, his little hands gripping the sash on Vivian's dress. He whimpered only slightly in his sleep. She spoke low as to not wake him.

"There's no place to hide Jack won't find us. I'd rather be with you. I'd rather be with Nan."

"Crow, Nat, Polly. Same goes for you. I don't want you kids hurt," said

Camille without looking at any of us. She merely stared ahead at the road in front of Johnny Sanders's ears.

Polly and Crow shook their heads. Camille didn't see it but took their meaning in the silence. There was a strange connection between us all. Even Vivian felt closer to me, and I'd only known her a tiny chunk of time. Maybe it was because we were all different. I wasn't as special as the rest, but being with them felt like home.

"I'm with you," I said to her.

Simple words could mean big things.

We reached the house by nightfall, and the sunflowers bloomed at our arrival. Nan was already standing outside the front door, a smile on her face and blue satin gloves on her hands. Somewhere on the wind behind her, I smelled an apple pie. Warm and inviting amnesia came with it as if the storm earlier wasn't as fresh as it had been a second ago.

Vivian's eyes lit up when she saw Nan, and she handed Jack Jr. to Polly so she could get down. We watched as Vivian ran to Nan, throwing her arms around her in an enthusiastic hug. Tears streamed down Vivian's face. She nestled her face in the blue, silk scarf around Nan's neck.

"There's my girl," said Nan. "My Vivvy girl. How I've missed you. I knew I'd see you again. My sweet, sweet girl."

"They are comin', Nan. They're comin' for us," said Vivian pulling away. "It's all my fault. I should never have left, and now they're comin' for us."

"No," said Camille jumping down from the wagon. "They're comin' because of me. It's my fault. I lost control."

"That's enough of that from the both of you. This day was comin' no matter what you did or didn't do. It always happens sooner or later. No point wallerin' in guilt and pity. We gotta prepare. Jacob says they'll be here by tomorrow evening."

Fear sent a shiver down my throat and into my belly. That warm amnesia blew away in the air around me. I swallowed hard several times but couldn't seem to wet my mouth properly. A silence passed between us full of foreboding. You didn't have to be Jacob to see a wicked wind was blowing our way.

In the middle of all the fear and doubt and guilt, a lovely thing happened. It was Polly who noticed it first. Such a small thing, but so full of beauty and hope when we needed it the most. I was helping her down from the wagon when she pointed to the side of the house. Camille had turned the snow off before our journey to the circus, but the snow drifts were still putting up a fight again the Texas weather.

There, in the highest drifts, the rose bushes stood tall and firm. The tiny buds had bloomed into beautiful, little roses. Pink ones with yellow on the underside of them. *A Better Tomorrow, Vivian's Rose*. Hope could spring even in the coldest circumstances.

Everyone went to bed readily after eating the dinner, and pie Nan had set out for us. After dinner, I was helping clear the dishes from the table. I glanced after Vivian carrying little Jack down the hall with Camille behind them. They seemed intent on a specific place, so I followed them to see where they were going.

The hallway was the one that led to my room and to Polly's room. A door appeared at the end of the hall from me. If pressed, I couldn't say I recognized a door had been there at all. Perhaps it had, and I never took note? That wasn't the smartest idea. I had searched up and down the hallway looking for other rooms. Most ended in bee stings or short retreats. Surely I would have tried that one had I seen it.

When I crept closer, I managed a better look inside without them noticing me. It turned out to be Vivian's room, decorated in floral wallpaper with birds that nested inside the drawings on the walls. They'd flutter here and there, bouncing from one picture to the next and chirping merrily as they went. The angels on Vivian smiled.

"It's just how I left it," she said absently.

"Well, there's one difference," said Camille pointing to a white crib in the corner. A mobile of birds and angels hung above it.

Vivian smiled in that way where something is nice but also hurts you too. A bittersweet smile holding back tears. She and Camille embraced like they had in the tent before. It was that way that made me uncomfortable to watch. It wasn't an ugly thing. The way they were together made me feel like I was watching something I shouldn't. It was a moment too intimate to be observed by someone uninvited. I bowed my head and left them alone. Silently, I made my way to my own room feeling terribly wretched.

Sleep did not come for me. I tried. Perhaps that was the problem. Trying to sleep rarely resulted in falling asleep. You either slept, or you didn't. Forcing my mind to quiet only seemed to make it work harder. I tossed and turned, trying to silence the din in my head, but every time I shut my eyes, all I could see was the angry mob. A sea of hatred reflected in the faces of normal folks. I saw Camille and the intense storm she created above and around herself. There was terror and fear and violence.

Finally, I gave up. There was nothing for it. The idea occurred to me to try the library. It had a comfortable charm and lots of soft places to doze. Maybe a change in scenery would ease my mind. I decided to give it a shot.

The house was quiet. Though I wore socks, every footstep I took on the old wooden floors sounded like it echoed across the hallways. I was thankful when I reached the cold study where it was carpeted, and my steps were muffled. Buck looked down at me as I entered.

"Aren't you supposed to be asleep?" he asked.

"Aren't you?" I countered.

"I am above sleep. Thus is the perfection of me."

"Well, good for you."

"Indeed. However, I would warn you not to go into the library at this time. It is occupied," he said regally.

"Occupied? By who?"

"Whom, dear boy. Whom. When speaking to me, you really should try using proper English."

"Alright. By *whom*?"

"Nan and Camille. I granted them permission to pass through my chambers. They are in there now plotting something. I don't know what. Frankly, eavesdropping is beneath me. However, if you were to do the eavesdropping, that would be appropriate. You are the level of creature for it anyway."

"And I 'spose you'd want to hear what it is I found out?" I asked. "But don't want to spy yourself."

"Spying is beneath me, of course," he said with his nose turned upwards.

"Of course."

"But I would be inclined to hear your transcription of it. Best to know the goings on around here. Not that it is of any consequence to me."

"And what do I get in return?"

"Well, I thought that was obvious. I'll let you pass without alerting them to your presence."

I sighed and looked up at him. Best to play along, I reckoned.

"Alright, you have a deal."

"Splendid," he said gesturing me forward with a flick of his antler.

As I approached the library door, I saw it was slightly ajar. A thin beam of light began at the door and spread outward in the darkness. When I peeked through, I saw Nan and Camille sitting next to one another, Nan in an armchair and Camille on a cushion on the floor. The older woman was stroking Camille's hair which had lost its colorful wrap. Shiny gloves moved like colored waves over and over again.

"I see you're worried," said Nan into Camille's hair.

"I...I was...I don't even know how to explain it."

"I tried to talk to Vivian, but she's..."

"I know I know," said Camille. "She was okay, but now, she's speaking in riddles. I can't get solid answer from her either anymore. Too much stress I 'spose. I forgot how she gets when that happens."

"I don't think she's speaking in riddles," replied Nan. "Sounded like plain English to me. She just wouldn't say much at all. The child is guarded."

"What I heard was nonsense. What did she tell you?"

"She told me there's a place beyond the shadows where no light can live. You can see everything there if you just try," said Nan gently.

"See what I mean? Riddles. I never was very good at deciphering her when she went down this road."

Camille let out a long sigh and looked down at the skirt of her dress. She hadn't changed when we got home. That drab outfit was crisp from rainwater dried in the open wind. Splatters of mud dotted in a way that almost looks like it was a pattern on the fabric. Bits of the bottom hem and her collar were singed from electricity.

"I did this to her, to all of us. It was bad, Nan. I didn't mean for it to get that bad."

"I know, honey. We all lose control sometimes," cooed Nan.

"But this was different. This was the bad old days. When I didn't know what I was doin'. No, I take it back. It was worse. It was so much more powerful out there. The storm I brought, it almost consumed me. All the power of it. I was so mad. I could have really hurt someone. Had Nat not stopped me, I might have hurt him too. I could have hurt the babies."

"But you didn't, dear. You stopped yourself. You are better than you think."

"I brought this trouble down on us, Nan. I should have left Viv there, but I just couldn't. Now? Now...I don't even know what will happen. What does Jacob say?"

Nan's hand paused for a second over Camille's hair. The hesitation said so much and so little at the same time. I couldn't see Nan's face, and I wasn't at all like Vivian, but I knew her thoughts all the same.

"Never mind what Jacob says. He isn't always right."

"Nan, please. If there's some way to work this so the children are safe, tell me. I have to protect them. My life doesn't matter, but I can't call forth the storms again. Not like that. I might not be able to stop myself next time. There has to be another way."

"There's always a way, child. You may not like it, but there is a way."

"What? What is it? I...I could lead the men away? I could let them chase me. No, that wouldn't save Vivian. Jake will surely search for her. Crow can fly away in the wagon with Polly and Nat. Nat's good enough with Johnny."

"Slow child. Those things won't save us all," Nan said to the space above Camille's head. "Even if you sent them away, where might they go? No safe places around here."

"You're right. Maybe the cloaking magic, like we do with the house. I could fashion some false people, and we could make them look like us. Let them beat us and whisk away Vivian and little Jack. They'd be taking some old bags. Wouldn't know it for days. Wait, no. They'd come back, and how would we get Jacob out? He won't go if you don't."

"Honey girl, you are missin' the obvious," interrupted Nan.

"Obvious? What am I missing?"

"Hold my hand," said Nan simply.

"No...no I won't do that. I can't do it, Nan. You know I can't."

"Camille..."

"I refuse that way, Nan. I won't do it. I'd rather die."

"You could protect them all so much better if you did. I've had my time as the keeper of this place. I've held onto it longer than most."

"I said no, and that's final. We'll find another way...somehow."

Chapter Twenty Seven

The following day was filled with work. Everyone had a job, and no one slacked at the tasks they were given. There was an urgency in the wind. None of us knew what was coming or when it would be here, but there was no doubting the dread we all felt.

When anyone looked at Jacob for answers, he refused to show us anything on his board. Nan had apparently ordered him to be silent for one reason or another. Vivian said little, neither in regular speech or riddles. I watched Polly sidle up to her once in the garden while admiring the snow roses. It was the only time all day I'd seen Vivian calm. She even smiled when she looked them over. There was only the tiniest sound as Polly approached her. She leaned in so close to Vivian, the fabric of her skirt brushed Polly's thin shoulder. She never touched Vivian though. Just stood next to her. Polly was a gentle soul. It was hard for anyone to deny her attention.

"Vivian? Can you see what's going to happen?"

Vivian paused as she reached down to touch one of her roses. She seemed to think a moment before gently stroking the pink and yellow petals. The angels on her arms had no expression. It was as if they were guarding their faces as well. They even collectively looked in another direction.

"I can't, little poppet. It's all too dark. Things will happen as they must."

We boarded up the house and braced the back door so the only way in or out was the front door. At first, that seemed wrong to me. Not giving us a way to escape out the back? What sense was that? Camille explained that they'd try to surround us that way, but if they saw a bolt back door, they would bother guarding it. Polly could move anyone she needed to through any wall, so we had as many exits as we needed.

It was sensible, and I was glad Camille's level head had returned to her. A solemn bit in the back of my mind mentioned something else. Camille had a solid plan because she'd prepared for this before. She had faced danger like this and was still frightened. It stole a little sturdiness from my knees. We could run of course, but we all knew only some of us came out alive in that scenario. Crow was the first to take that option off the table. None of us argued. Leaving would mean leaving Nan and Jacob too. Nan was too old, and Jacob was stuck in his chair. It wasn't an option even before it was discussed.

All day long we braced for the coming night. All. Day. Long. Food didn't taste like anything at all. Every creak in the floorboard spooked us. The slightest wind had me jumping like a jackrabbit. I finally decided to stand guard at the point where the main road met the path to the house, right where the sign for *Camille's Home for Wayward Children* stood.

I wasn't sure what was worse, dealing with danger or waiting for it to come to you. My old pistol was heavy in my hand. There still were no bullets for it, but it was better than nothing. Before I had come out to stand watch, I checked the library again, hoping one of the books might reveal something to me. Any sort of knowledge or maybe a kind of weapon. But the pages were as blank for me as they'd always been. I was as useless as the unloaded gun I held at my side.

The sunflowers told me they were coming before I ever saw the headlights. It was nearly nightfall, twilight to be specific. Those beautifully tall flowers bloomed radiantly next to me, almost craning their petals in my direction. All of a sudden, they shriveled in their spot. With a small shudder, their yellow heads rotted and crumbled to ashes beneath the sign. In the distance, I could hear the faintest sound of automobiles in the darkening horizon.

There was nothing to do but run and shout. Nothing left but to warn the others. By the time I made it to the house, nearly everyone was out front, looking at me with terror. I struggled to catch my breath.

"They're coming," I managed to spit out before ragged inhales.

"How long?" asked Camille.

"Not long. Twenty minutes maybe."

The fear disappeared from her face. She suddenly had a purpose now; we all did. Camille stood up straight and turned to the rest of the crew.

"It's time now. Nothin' for it. Polly, you and Crow take little Jack Jr. down to Nan's room. He'll be safest there. Vivian will stay up top with me in the kitchen. I need you and Jacob to tell which way to go next. Nat, you'll go with Polly and stay out of sight."

"The hell I will," I said standing up as tall as I could.

"Listen Galahad, we ain't got time…"

"No, he has to stay," said Vivian suddenly looking at Camille and then over toward me. Her eyes were sadder than anything else like she knew something about this I didn't. "He has to stay up top with us. That's how it goes."

"Alright, not arguin' anymore about that," said Camille shaking her head. "Polly, you good with keeping the baby?"

Polly held her breath and nodded. I could tell she was trying really hard to stiffen her spine and be brave, a real witch. She took the baby in her arms and pulled the blanket tighter around his arms for the comfort of it. It wasn't hard to tell she desperately needed someone to do the same to her. I wanted so badly to hug her myself.

"Crow, you gonna stay with Polly? If things go bad, you two take the baby and make your way to the barn. Take Johnny Sanders and go south, understand?"

He nodded, holding a knife in his hand. A small part of me shivered inside as Polly inched closer to Crow, taking his worn hand in hers. Their eyes met in a tender way that made me want to look somewhere else. I didn't of course, and I tried very hard to measure the amount of heat burning behind my eyes.

Polly spoke very quietly with Crow; barely loud enough for me to hear.

"You don't have to, you know," she said.

"I do not have to what?"

"Stay with me. Protect me and little Jack. I can do it. I can get him away to safety."

"I know."

"You're a bird. I don't think anyone would blame you if you flew away. You could go find some of Camille's friends. Get help. Stay with them."

"No, I have flown enough," he said simply. "It is time to stay. Birds fly away. Men stay. I will not leave any of you."

CHAPTER TWENTY EIGHT

We had just made it inside with everyone in their places when the men came in their trucks. As Camille predicted, they did a good lap around the house to see if there was any other way for us to escape. After seeing there wasn't, a group of six trucks full of angry farmers pulled into the front driveway. More than thirty men poured out of the vehicles holding shotguns, pistols, and torches. Doors slammed, and people hooted and hollered. A buzzing followed them, like the angry din of a hive of bees.

Camille, Vivian, Jacob, and I watched them in between the boards over the windows. We had extinguished all light in the house, hoping it would be enough cover. I recognized Jack as he leapt off the back of one of the trucks. The stocky man was right beside him. There were several townspeople I remembered following Jack, including the chicken man who gave me a ride to Tanglewood so long ago. That gripped my lungs a little.

My gut fell into my shoes when the final truck unloaded. It was a large truck, normally used for hauling feed and hay. Inside were at least a dozen men lead by none other than Polly's father, Elder Jones, the man in the black suit. His cohorts dressed just like him and lined up behind them like a practiced army. Our enemies had rallied.

"Camille Lavendou!" shouted Jack two feet from the front porch. "You need to come out now. Seems to me you have been collectin' things that ain't yours. Surrender yourself and the people you took, and these fine gentlemen might just let you live."

A cheer let out around him. There was banter back and forth, one trying to top the others as to a fitting punishment for her. None seemed keen on the idea of her living. Even fewer like the idea of her body staying in one piece.

"Is Jack persuading them again?" I asked.

"No," said Viv. "He don't have to with these fellas."

A lanky figure emerged in front of the others.

"I do not see why we must mince words," said Elder Jones as he strode elegantly into the spotlight next to Jack, his suit finely pressed. "I have been speakin' with this fine gentleman here, Miss Lavendou, and it seems you are in a bit of a pickle. Your fine friends in Amarillo are nowhere near to help you. However, if you give me back my daughter and this man's family, we will spare your house and the rest of its residents. We are not in the business of killing children. If you do this without protest and in a civil manner, you might live long enough to see your home again. If not…"

Elder Jones held his hand out to seemingly no one. In a flash, one of his men placed a stick of wood wrapped in soaked cloth. With a flick of a match, the torch caught, illuminating the menace in the man in black's eyes.

"You have to the count of three, Miss Lavendou. One…" said Elder Jones.

"Camille, we can't just let him…" I tried to say.

"Hush, child. I'm thinking," she snapped.

"Two…"

"Just bring on the storm. Wash them away, Camille," I pleaded.

"No Nat. I can't do it again."

"Three!"

Elder Jones waited for a second for some sort of answer. When he got none, he flicked the torch against the house. It was so effortless, this action. Without a second thought, this man threw a lit torch at a house that held his daughter, hoping it would catch.

I couldn't help but grin like a devil when it didn't. His torch hit the wall of the house, immediately extinguished itself, and fell lifeless to the ground. All that remained of its threat was the acrid smell of a flame snuffed out. A biting flash and then nothing at all, like when you blew out a match.

I drank in every astonished look on every one of their faces. It didn't take them long to rally though. Every man ran to light more and more torches, most makeshift from bits of old fence and the legs of chairs. A melee of fire rained down on the front of the house. Each one blew out before catching on anything. There was a debris field of dead torches lining the porch.

"See, gentleman?" said Elder Jones while waving his hands in the air like he was conducting a sermon. "I have told you the dangers of sufferin' a witch to live. Now you see with your own eyes the devil's work she has done here."

The men raged behind him. Hatred rose in the mouths of mortals louder and faster than I thought possible. They ran at the house with hatchets and pickaxes, intent on breaking inside. Jack and Elder Jones stood aside as the stocky man ran up the porch stairs with an axe.

He swung the thing as hard as he could into the bolted front door only to fall backward, clutching his arm. The collision made a loud clang when metal touched the wood of the house. His weapon fell next to him, the blade bent to the side and warped like it was made of wax instead of steel. The man howled in pain.

Elder Jones narrowed his eyes at the house and pointed one, long finger at the door.

"Witchcraft! Gentleman, tear this place apart. We will have back what is rightfully ours and cleanse this place of the devil."

Men ran to the porch with whatever weapons they could find. Hatchets, pickaxes, saws, and hammers. We crouched beside Jacob in his little chair by the window wincing at every slam and knock on the wall. I tried once to pull Jacob down off the chair he was sitting in. He would be so much safer down on the floor with us.

The boy wouldn't budge. It wasn't from his own fighting. I pulled and pulled on him, but it was as if his bottom was stuck to the chair. His britches seemed glued in place. He waved me away with a sad look. There was no moving him.

"Camille, we have to do something. What if they get in here?" I whispered.

"Just stay put, child. When they realize none of their tricks will work to get 'em in here, they'll give up."

"What about Jacob?" I asked.

I hadn't done it on purpose. There was nothing magical about it really. For some reason, the minute I asked about Jacob, a shadow fell over the window where he sat. The silhouette of an evil man loomed over us and silenced me.

We watched helplessly as he squatted down and peered through the space in between the planks we nailed the window shut, the same space we'd been using to spy on the mob from the kitchen. Jacob trembled as one grey eye peeked through the planks and rested right on his face.

"Well well," said Jack from the other side of the window. "I think I found a way inside."

There was the unmistakable sound of someone pulling back the hammer of a gun. The man's silhouette faded a little, and the eye disappeared, only to be replaced by the barrel of a pistol. Jacob shut his eyes and braced himself.

Camille and I were up in a flash. Within seconds, she had thrown up the bolt and stepped out onto the porch, a vision of green and purple silk on the wind. Despite their bluster, the men all stepped back, even stumbling back onto the lawn. Camille stood tall without a lick of fear on her face. She was an immovable statue and a rare sight in an angry evening.

"I do believe someone was asking after me," she said loudly, staring down Jack in front of the window.

He smiled as he stood up, uncocking his gun and raising it above his head. I tried to run out with her, but Vivian grabbed me and pulled me back inside. We scrambled a bit as she scooted in front of the door, bracing it with her body. The angels on her arms silently wailed in fear.

"We can't just leave her out there!" I yelled at her, trying to move her out of the way.

"I don't like it either, but she made me promise to keep you from doing this very thing!"

"Vivian, she could die!"

"You saw what happened at the circus. Camille can handle herself," she said.

"She nearly killed herself and everyone else."

"Stay, kid. Just for now. I won't keep you here long. I can't. Just hold off, alright?"

It wasn't what I wanted, but it was either argue with Vivian or watch what was happening with Jacob. Seeing what was going on was more important, so I joined Jacob by the window. We could see Camille. She was standing with her fists on her hips staring down over thirty armed men. Every inch of me wanted to go out and help her. My legs twitched with the need to run.

"We were asking for you, witch," said Elder Jones. "You have stolen our children; this man's whole family. What say you to these charges?"

"I say y'all are a bunch of strong, strong men. Look at you. How many we got here? Whoa, too many for a little ole witch like me to count. How dangerous you must think I am to need this many grown men to take me down. I must be up there with the best of them."

"Do not stall, witch. Just give us the children," said Elder Jones.

"And tell me where mine are!" shouted the stocky man from the ground. A few men had pulled him aside to tend to his arm. "The white-haired ones. What did you do with 'em?'"

"I took no children. I take no one. I offer a home and shelter and knowledge to those you throw away. You, sir, used two babies you found in a burnt out hovel as a sideshow attraction to help peddle your potions," she said pointing at the stocky man.

She looked over to Elder Jones, holding him with her dark eyes. He tried not to move but flinched anyway under her scrutiny.

"Your daughter you seem so upset about? You were ready to sell her off to a man four times her age to win his favor. When she didn't want to go, you chained her to a post. And just now, you threw a flamin' torch at the very house she is hiding in."

To her left was Jack, smiling like a snake. She faced him as well.

"You used your own brand of magic to lure Vivian away from her home. Threatened to kill your own baby if she tried to run. Forced her to work your run-down circus. If you gonna call out a witch, best name yourself too."

"Magic? What magic?" asked Elder Jones turning his eyes on Jack.

"Oh, didn't you know? Jack over here dabbles in his own brand of magic, the hypocrite that he is," she said turning to him with a smug half-smile. "Poor poor Jack. Must be pretty hard knowing magic was the only thing keepin' her with you. Funny though, ain't it? The second she saw me, she came runnin'. No magic needed. I wonder what I have you don't."

It was the first time since they showed up I saw Jack lose his self-satisfied grin. It was almost comical how it fell, like one of the movie villains. What seemed comical one second turned positively frightening the next. I felt Vivian tremble next to me.

"Please don't do it, Cam. Don't turn that dial," whispered Vivian to herself.

"Oh that's right," continued Camille edging closer and closer to him. "Viv told me all about what you're missin'. Maybe I should enlighten your fellows here."

A rage overtook the man, and he lunged for her. Camille didn't move an inch. She merely raised her hands a gust of wind sprang from nowhere and blasted Jack and the other men off the porch and onto their backsides in the grass.

There was no struggle this time. Vivian and I scrambled to our feet and ran out of the front door. The frenzy in the air was unmistakable. No more talking, no more holding back. The mob would try to rush her, and we couldn't sit back and watch it happen.

I made it to Camille just as Jack got to his feet. He was almost to her when I stepped in front and raised my gun to his face. The hammer cocked, and the sound stopped him for a second. It stopped everyone. Dozens of temporary surrenders. We all breathed in the sweat and anxiety in the night air. Somewhere, off in the distance in the dark, I spied them. Two boxcar men watching us. They were just a bit familiar. Both dirty, both bloody. One had mismatched shoes, and the other had no shoes at all.

My breath caught, but I tried to focus on Jack in front of me. In a flash, the men were gone. It wasn't like they ran off. The just flickered away. I was alone again standing there on the porch with my pistol pointing at Jack's face wondering if they were real or ghosts.

"You want me to bring 'em back? I can do that. They came for you," whispered a voice in my head.

"What? What did you say?" I asked trying to see who had spoken to me. Jack's mouth hadn't moved. At least, I didn't think it had. The terrible words must have come from that secret place where Jack kept all his persuasions.

"I said what do you think you're doin', kid?" asked Jack.

"I'm gonna shoot you if you take another step," I retorted trying very hard to sound bigger than I was.

"I remember you," he said. "The brave kid. Why don't you lower that pistol, and let us take the darky, son? I could use a man like you 'round the circus. I can tell you like Vivian and my boy. You could keep an eye on them, even visit your little girlfriend too if Elder Jones allows it. Things could be easier fer you."

There was that little voice in my head again like when we were at the circus. Just like I heard it only moments ago. The voice that told you to do things; things you didn't want to do.

"Just put it down, kid. No one would blame you. Let us have her, and we'll give you anything you want."

"Cut that crap out, moron," I said suddenly adapting Camille's brazen way of speaking. "Your tricks don't work on me. Back off or I'll turn your head into a train tunnel."

It was almost funny how angry his face got. Up close, I saw the place on the bridge of his nose where I had broken it. His skin was puffy and purple. When his whole face reddened, it made that knot flame like an angry boil.

I held my gun on him as Camille put her hand on my shoulder. Vivian was clinging to her back, and they started leading me step by step back toward the front door.

"This is what's gonna happen," I said looking at all the men while still training my gun on Jack. "We are gonna go back inside, and y'all are going to get back to your trucks and leave this place. If you don't, I will shoot this man, and Camille will finish off the rest of you."

Every step back we took, Jack took a slow step forward. He was following us like a circling buzzard, a very hungry look in his eyes. We were nearly to the door when I couldn't stand it anymore.

"Back off or I will shoot you!"

"Oh is that so? How you gonna do that with no bullets, kid?" said Jack, flashing that grin of his again.

Everything strong inside me went soggy. In that terrible moment, it was as if time stood still. A tiny voice inside me told me this was the time. I'd lived on this Earth until now, but this would be where it all ended. If there was no hope to survive, I just had to take as many as could down with me.

The three of us turned and tried to make a break for the door only to run straight into Elder Jones. He was standing in the doorway, looming over us. In our haste to get to Camille, Vivian and I had left the door open. There wasn't even time to scream.

A tangle of hands fell on me. Some were friendly, Vivian and Camille trying to grab me, to hold me close to them. Most were not, rough farmer hands tearing at my clothes and shoving me around. They were trying to pry us apart. I kicked and scratched at as many as I could. After a while, it was hard to tell who was friend or foe.

As we fought to stay together, in one piece, I thought about the boxcar men who I forced to jump from the train. The ones I saw in the dark horizon. The pain I'd forced on them. Now, I was getting mine. They had been haunting my thoughts, and now I would pay my debt. It didn't mean I had to do it willingly, but it was coming all the same.

Everything stopped not with a gunshot, not with a death, but with an old woman yelling the most implausible thing over the cacophony of anger.

"See here now, I have gifts for you all, and if you don't let those folks alone, you won't get 'em. Would be your loss for sure."

It was so absurd they couldn't help but stop pulling on us. The arms held on but they didn't hurt anymore, just held us in place. I was so thankful to fall back into a hug with Camille again, I didn't care why they ceased hurting us. Vivian wrapped her arm around my chest. Her angels were silently whimpering against my shirt.

We all looked toward the porch where Nan stood, her arms full of canvases. Her red satin gloves pinched and creased around the stacks she carried. She had the most implausible smile on her face. No one said a word. No one moved. It was all just so strange no one could. Even Camille gawked at her.

"Let's see here, oh yes, Mr. Coffrey," she said walking up to the stocky man still holding his arm. "This is for you. It's your brother, Anthony."

Nan handed him a canvas. It was one of her ghostly paintings, the ones she did of the people who died and wanted to be remembered. The portrait of Anthony gazed out at the stocky man like it had gazed out at me. At first, I thought it was a trick, some ruse Nan had planned out, but then I saw his reaction. The stocky man recognized the ghost in the painting. It was written all over his face. The likeness was remarkable. The brothers even had the same chin. Tears well up in his eyes as he stared at his twin.

"Tony. This is Tony…but he died."

"Yes, dear," said Nan patting him on the shoulder. "That's why this one is for you."

She hobbled in her layers of clothing over to another man and held a painting out for him to take. He dropped the axe in his hand and took the canvas with shaking fingers.

"Your wife Margery, I believe. Yes? Such a lovely soul," cooed Nan as she made her way to the next person.

One after another, she handed portraits out to the men in the crowd. She moved slowly but with purpose. A small, hunched woman, glided around the angry mob like a ghost herself. Each portrait doused the flames of their anger. Each time it made them tremble and even weep. Each one turned into guilty schoolboys in front of her.

"Mr. Samson, your daughter Midge. And Mr. Daughtry, your mother, Enid. She was exceptionally chatty when I painted this one."

I was so tense I barely noticed we weren't being held anymore. The rough hands had gone slack, too enamored with Nan to remember what they were doing. Some men had moved away to place themselves in the old woman's path to see if she had anything for them. Even Jack had released my shirt if only for a moment.

There was a gentle sound of weeping on the porch, a girl weeping. It hadn't been audible at first, but with all the tumult melting, the girl made her presence known. We turned to see Polly walking out of the front door, Crow holding Jack Jr. behind her. Vivian ran to them, grabbing the baby and holding him to her chest. Camille and I moved to join them.

Polly was holding a portrait, but I couldn't see the front of it. She walked over to where her father stood. Her little fingers trembled as she held the canvas. Polly's weeping stayed steady as she came up behind the lanky man. He was busy watching Nan in astonishment, so he didn't see her at first.

"Daddy?" she asked in a heartbreakingly small voice.

Elder Jones turned to see his daughter holding a painting, tears rolling down her cheeks. What started out as an innocent gaze turned mean and accusatory in seconds. It seemed the more she cried, the angrier she got. Polly turned the painting to face her father, and there, painted just as ghostly as the rest, was Luke. The dead boy in the painting was her brother, and he came to Nan because he didn't want to be forgotten.

"You killed him, Daddy? You killed Luke? You killed him!"

Elder Jones panicked. He started jittering about like a skittish bird. A lot of the men turned to look at the spectacle, the ones from his colony included. No longer was he the feared Elder in a sermon. A man above all others. Evil men fall to mud just like anyone else. The only difference is they belong there.

"Hush now, child. You don't know what you are saying. These are only lies the witch woman told you. Luke is..."

"Dead! He's dead! You killed my brother!"

Polly dropped the painting on the ground and began hitting and kicking her father. It didn't do much damage given his size, but it was bringing a lot of attention to him. I thought about intervening but stopped. He was trying to stop her but not hurting her. The fire had gone out of him as much as it had everyone else. Besides, this was Polly's demon, and she had a right to beat him herself.

"I didn't..." he tried blocking her fists.

"Liar!"

"I didn't...mean to! He was helping you. I know he helped you with your little plot. I had no choice. He had to be punished. He had to atone. I didn't mean to leave him out in the dust storm. I didn't know it would be so bad."

He tried to grab her wrists, to stop her from fighting him, but his hands kept running through her. Confused, he tried to grab her shoulders, and his hands went right through her small body. Polly stopped hitting him long enough stare a hole into his eyes. For the first time, he looked genuinely afraid of his daughter. He couldn't touch her anymore. He couldn't hurt her.

Elder Jones stumbled backward trying to get away from her, but Polly socked him right in the gut. He fell backward off the porch and hit the ground hard, sputtering and coughing as he struggled to get to his feet. She turned and ran into Crow's waiting arms, crying on his shoulder. When her father got up and tried to come after her, Crow merely pointed his knife at the man and held it there.

"Not another step. You will be sorry."

When Elder Jones continued to step forward. With one arm still around Polly, Crow threw the knife, and it stuck in the man's shoe, pinning his now bleeding foot to the baseboards of the porch. He wailed and tried to pull the knife out of his foot. It wouldn't budge. The more he struggled, the more his foot bled. Elder Jones reached out to his daughter.

Crow looked down at Polly, and they both nodded. He balled himself up and became a bird, leaving a mess of clothes where he just stood. After he perched on Polly's shoulder, she walked steadily over to her father still pinned to the floor.

"Please! Please child. Help me!"

Her little hands were sweaty fists at her sides. I'd never seen her look so angry. There was a darkness in her eyes, a shadow. I recognized it, unfortunately. It happened to me once, but I never wanted it for her. She wore the shadow one gets when a loved one is stolen.

Right when he made his last plea to her, Polly spat in his face and pulled the knife from his foot. Her father screamed again when she did.

"Thank you. Thank you for helping me," he said, wiping the spit from his forehead.

"It isn't for you," she said through her teeth. "This is my friend's knife. I said I'd give it back to him. It's worth more than you are."

Polly and Crow made their way back over to us in silence. No one moved.

Nan now stood in the middle of a crowd of men. Moments ago, they were hateful wretches, and now, they stood around idle holding portraits of their lost loved ones. Even Elder Jones tried to take the portrait of his son Polly dropped, but Vivian stormed over and snatched it away before he could, all of her angels scowling at him.

There was only one man left who was unconvinced. That, of course, was Jack.

"Not another step, witch," he said closing the gap between him and Nan with his pistol raised to her chest. "You may have fooled these idiots, but you haven't fooled me."

"I have fooled no one. I don't use that sort of magic. Trivial really. I merely gave these people back a piece of what they lost."

"Oh yeah? And what about what I lost? You took my wife and child."

"Come now Jack, we all know Viv, and the boy are merely trophies to you," said Nan as she carefully began removing her gloves. "What you lost no one can give back to you."

"Oh no," whispered Camille next to me. "No no no no no."

Camille's eyes went wide, and I knew something was about to happen. She started moving toward them, and I followed.

"You think you're so sharp, old woman. If you're so smart, what is it I lost?"

"Why your innocence, dear boy," said Nan with a sympathetic smile. "All those wretched things the foreman's son made you do. Just terrible. Such indecencies should never be visited upon anyone, especially someone so young. It's no wonder you persuade people into staying with you the way you do. It wouldn't do to be the victim again, would it?"

The world ceased turning as the air dropped. No other way to describe it. All of the air fell away and left nothing for anyone else to breathe. Jack's face was full of pain and shock, the deadliest combination if there ever was one. Once the shock wears off, all that's left is pain and insurmountable rage.

I just couldn't get there in time. There was nothing Camille or I could do. Jack pulled the trigger, and Nan went down. That gentle smile never left her face. Jack just stood there dumbfounded as she fell, a red flower of blood blooming on her chest. She hit the ground with a padded thud, her layers of clothes spread all around her.

I got to her first, skidding the last few feet on my knees in the grass. Nan reached for me, that sweet grin of her seeking me out with her kind eyes. I grabbed her hands, marveling at how they looked. I'd never seen them without gloves on.

Her skin was cooling fast under my touch. I didn't know what to do.

"Help me! Won't somebody help me? Somebody do something!" I screamed in the darkness.

Everyone stood frozen watching me. No one helped, no one tried. Vivian whispered something in one of the men's ears. Whatever she said spurred him into action. He gathered some of the men, and they grabbed Jack and Elder Jones. Neither said a word as their hands were bound and they were led away to the trucks. No one struggled. No one fought. All the anger had turned to fear and regret, and the mob was making a sheepish retreat.

Camille stood just behind me, looking down at us both with the strangest gaze. She focused in on the red staining the front of Nan's dress and then at our hands holding tight to one another.

"Oh…god," was all she could utter.

"Nat," whispered Nan, looking up at me. "Look at me, child."

She raised her hand and touched it to my cheek. I felt a warm sensation where she touched me, like something had been wiped there. When I checked with my hand, there was paint on my fingers. That didn't seem possible, and at first, I thought it was the trick of firelight, but when I looked at the places on my hands where she touched me, I saw paint smears there too. They were smudges of brown and plum, the colors of Nan's skin.

The goddess painted with the colors of the old gods.

"It's been so long since I touched anyone," she mused while slipping away from me.

I grabbed at her shoulders and hands. I held them tightly, thinking holding her tighter would keep her from dying.

"Nan, please don't go. Please. I need you. The books won't talk to me remember? You have to stay to help me. I don't know what to do without you. This isn't home if you leave. Please, you have to stay. You can't go now."

I tried to swallow back the tears, but they just came. There was no stopping them. Wet brine fell from my cheeks and splashed down on her. It collected where I held her hand, rinsing her color from my skin, washing her away with it.

"Nan, please don't go," I whispered through the tears.

"Oh child, don't cry. You'll just ruin the flowers."

She went still then, her eyes shutting in front of me. I grabbed her hand harder, trying to keep her from drifting away, but it was too late. Nan was already gone. Nothing could stop me now. No reason to hold back. I cried over her body. I wailed like a child, and as I did, the world cried with me. A steady torrent of water fell from the sky and rained down on us. It soaked me and covered Nan, washing away all her pretty paint in the process.

Somehow in the midst of it all, I heard Vivian and Camille behind me. Their voices were somber and brimming with tears of their own.

"She can't be gone. Not like this," said Vivian.

"I think this is exactly how she wanted it," retorted Camille, sniffling with a tint of sour in her words.

"I was off a little I guess," said Vivian in a sort of daze. "I guess I have you to thank for that."

"What do you mean?" asked Camille.

"I predicted the rain in two days. This one's a bit early."

"Don't look at me," said Camille. "This one ain't mine."

CHAPTER TWENTY NINE

It took a long time for me to sit up and look around at the world again. All the men were gone, having stolen away in the rain. Polly and Crow held one another on the porch. He was clothed once again and looking out at me with concern. Vivian and Jack Jr. stood just behind Camille as she knelt a foot away from me. The downpour had only just relented after I stopped crying, and everyone was drenched.

"Come on now, Nat. Time to stand up, alrighty?" said Camille.

"But Nan? Her body?"

"She is of the earth, child. Nan will be one with it by morning. It's the way things work with her. Nothing to do about it right now 'cept go inside and get some dry clothes on."

I got off my knees and struggled to my feet. Camille urged me on without reaching a hand out to help me. It was odd, how she kept her distance. Even when I began walking back toward the house, I noticed she was careful not to touch my bare skin. She rested one hand gently on my shoulder but always over my shirt.

The energy between us had changed. She felt far away. It made me nervous. Camille was still kind but wary for some reason or another like I might be dangerous. The slightest twitch of movement made her overreact.

"I think we should bury her," I said.

"Hush now, Galahad. We can worry about that in the mornin'. I promise you it will be alright," said Camille.

Vivian hurried on ahead of us and ushered Crow and Polly inside. She was whispering something in a rush, but I couldn't understand what it was. All I saw was a set of confused faces before they were hurried inside. Camille continued to guide me forward with a very careful hand.

"What's going on?" I asked.

"I understand why you ask that. This next bit is gonna get a little weird," replied Camille.

"What do you mean by *weird*?"

"I'm gonna warn you about what will be in that kitchen. Jacob won't be there anymore. Be prepared for that part."

"Why? Why won't Jacob be there? Did one of the men get him?"

"No. Not that. Remember the story I told you about the goddess and the child?" Camille asked.

"The gods split the goddess in two. A child who is the anchor that keeps the goddess from floating away into the stars."

"Yes, that's it exactly. Jacob and Nan. Now that she's gone, Jacob is gone too," said Camille as gently as she could.

I stopped in my tracks and looked at her, searching her eyes for the slightest hint of a lie. This had to be a joke, a very bad one at that. There was no flicker in Camille's eyes that said she was lying. Jacob was Nan's child? He was gone too? I thought there was nothing left inside me to hurt, but I was wrong.

"But Jacob is a boy, and Nan's a girl," I argued.

"Is she?"

"Was she not?"

"Gods aren't concerned with trivial things like boys and girls, men and women. It's not such a line in the sand. Nan started this world as a boy, and became whatever it is she wanted."

"But…but I thought she was immortal. I thought she couldn't be killed," I pleaded.

"The only way to kill her is to touch her. You touched her. I'm so sorry, sweet boy."

My jaw hung open. As if this night could get any worse.

"You mean, she would have lived if I hadn't touched her? She could have healed from the gunshot."

"You didn't know. It's not your fault."

"How is this not my fault?" I asked, raising my voice.

Anger welled inside me. None of this made any sense at all. I wanted to die too. I wanted to fall inside a deep dark hole and never come up for air. I clenched my hands in fists and stomped the ground as hard as I could. To my surprise, the earth rumbled when I did like thunder in the ground. The world trembled for a moment under my foot. Camille and I wobbled for a moment to regain our balance.

I released my fists and looked up at her with the sudden knowledge that I had made that happen. My anger had moved the ground. I clenched my first and squeezed hard, focusing all my hurt beneath me. The ground shuddered beneath us until I relaxed.

"I did that?"

"Yes," she said carefully replacing her hand on my shoulder. "Yes child, you did. There's a part to the story we didn't explain. The goddess always dies when she decides she wants to. When she chooses the next in line. There was a long line before Nan, and there'll be a long line after her."

"What does that mean? Camille, what's happening to me?"

"She took off her gloves, Nat. She reached out for you. You are the next in line."

"No…no…no I can't do this. I don't know the first thing about…"

"Just breathe, child. Nothing has to be figured out tonight. We have plenty of time to learn what all this means for you. You are here as long as you want, just don't let anyone touch your skin. Don't worry. Vivian's telling the others right now."

She started guiding me back toward the house again, and I went along without knowing how to do anything else. I couldn't be immortal. I couldn't be the goddess. There was no way I could replace Nan.

We were at the front door now that lead into the kitchen. I paused there trying to wrap my brain around the fact when we walked inside, there would be no Jacob sitting there. He had been a constant fixture in the kitchen since I first arrived at the house. It would be strange without him. The place would feel so hollow. First Nan and now Jacob.

"It's going to be strange seeing an empty chair when we go inside," I said to Camille.

She looked at me with a tired smile.

"Honey, I don't think this is quite hittin' you yet. You are like the goddess in the story now. Nan had her child self in the form of Jacob fixed to that chair. He was her anchor. When we walk into that door, there will be the child form of you in that chair. It's the way things work. A young Nathaniel, all knobby-kneed and scuffed up from playing with toads and other boys things. He's gonna be in there takin' Jacob's place. Your anchor."

"Wait what?"

Panic shot through me. I wasn't expecting this. It had to be a mistake. Nothing made sense to me. There was no way the child version of me was going to be sitting at that chess set. That just wasn't possible.

"Come on now, I'm anxious to meet him. I can't wait to see how cute you were as a little boy," said Camille hurrying ahead of me and waving at me to follow her.

"No, Camille wait. I…I have to explain. Please don't."

I tried to run after her, but it was too late. By the time I got inside the kitchen, everyone was already there staring at the little table where Jacob had been less than an hour ago. No one spoke. A few times, Polly gazed up at me with a shocked look on her face. Vivian's face was hiding her true feelings, but her angels stared in slack-jawed wonderment. Even Crow seemed confused. Camille, being Camille, smile wryly at the person in Jacob's chair and then back at me. She beckoned me forward, and I took the last few steps into the kitchen to face the newest resident of *Camille's House for Wayward Children*. My child anchor.

It had been so long since I'd seen that version of me. When we locked eyes, the exact same eyes, it sent shivers down my spine. In front of me was the eight-year-old version of myself I'd lost years ago. The one who lived with Mamaw on the farm. Mamaw who braided my hair and tied in it little ribbons even though I didn't like it. She'd insist on making me dresses from the prettily patterned flour sacks she bought at the general store. My Mamaw who always had held onto an over-inflated sense of hope I'd grow into liking pretty things like other girls. She'd even cut up lace doilies to fashion some trim to the edges of dress sleeves as if that would help matters.

I stared at the eight-year-old girl that had been me and let out a breath I didn't know I was holding. There was no fighting it anymore. No hiding what I once was. My shoulders slumped in defeat. When my child anchor smiled wide, showing that two teeth were missing, I gave up. I waved at her, and she waved back with such enthusiasm it hurt me to watch.

"Well," said Camille with a knowing bounce in her voice. "It seems you've been keeping a secret from us, Nathaniel. Apparently, your real name is Natalie."

"I just...I was gonna tell you, Camille..."

"Save it, child. Around here, your past doesn't matter. You have been Galahad since the day I met you, and that's not gonna change one bit."

About the Author

Michelle Rene is a creative advocate and the author of a number of published works of science fiction, historical fiction, humor and everything in between. She has won a number of indie book awards for her historical and speculative fiction, including Chanticleer Reviews' Best Book of the Year for 2017.

When not writing, she is a professional artist and all around odd person. She lives as the only female with her husband, son, and ungrateful cat in Dallas, Texas.

Thank you so much for reading one of our **Fantasy** novels.
If you enjoyed our book, please check out our recommended title for your
next great read!

War of the Staffs by Steve Stephenson & K.M. Tedrick

"Offers an enjoyable romp for high fantasy fans." *–KIRKUS REVIEWS*

View other Black Rose Writing titles at www.blackrosewriting.com/books

and use promo code **PRINT** to receive a **20% discount** when purchasing.